D
A C(

EIGHT CHILLING WINTER MYSTERIES

Edited by
Jess Faraday

Contributions by
Leonhard August, Emily Baird,
Cris de Borja, Mark Hague,
Christalea McMullin, Lee Mullins,
Kirk VanDyke, Wendy Worthington

Artwork by
Virginia Cantarella

ELM BOOKS, 2012
Laramie, Wyoming

12/25/2012

Dear Mom & Dad, thank you so much for
making this book possible!! Lots of love,
Seila

Death on a Cold Night edited by Jess Faraday
Copyright © 2012 by Elm Books

ISBN: 978-0-9886116-0-3 (E-Format)
ISBN: 978-0-9886116-1-0 (Paperback)

Elm Books
1175 State Highway 130
Laramie, WY 82070
(http://elm-books.com)

Cover and illustrations by Virginia Cantarella
(http://www.virginiacantarella.com)

Typeface: Cochin (usually)

Printed by:
Mirasmart
1010 Hanley Industrial Court
Brentwood, MO 63144

CONTENTS

FOREWORD

A MYSTERY IS a story that revolves around a crime and its solution. Since Edgar Allan Poe popularized the detective story in the 19th century, the genre has expanded to include a wide range of setups and situations, from the cozy, represented here by Cris de Borja's *A Theft of Teapots*, to the ripped-from-the-headlines crime stories exemplified by Lee Mullins' *Burnt December.*

Sleuths, also, come in many forms: a precocious child, like the narrator of *Death Benefits* by Emily Baird; an unemployed person marking time on public transport, like the protagonist of Mark Hague's *In the Public Eye*; Kirk VanDyke's mountain cabin caretaker in *The Afternoon of the Storm*; or a quick-thinking assistant movie producer, like the main character of Wendy Worthington's story, *Snow in Winter.*

Over the last decade or so, there has been a trend toward including supernatural elements in mystery fiction, as well as other genres. We have included two excellent examples for your reading pleasure, whether your tastes run to vampires (Christalea McMullin's *Club Pandemonium*) or toward Native American legends come to life (Leonhard August's *Storm of Mystery.*)

Each of these stories has been hand-picked to provide a taste of the many different kinds of stories that can be described as 'mystery,' as well as to form a harmonious and complimentary collection. We have also strived to reflect the diversity that is our world today. We do hope you will enjoy this volume.

Jess Faraday, November 2012

SNOW IN WINTER

by

Wendy Worthington

IT WAS JANUARY, and it was snowing. It took me a moment to realize why that was strange. It wasn't the snow itself. It was the fact that it was snowing in Los Angeles, and it wasn't a movie effect. It wasn't that soap-bubble thing after the Christmas parade at Disneyland. This was real snow. You could stick your tongue out and catch a flake and not choke on a chemical concoction.

It didn't last, of course. Snow this low down in a desert is unnatural, and even Los Angeles can only handle so much peculiarity. But the snow was what made me pay attention to another thing I would otherwise have taken for granted. Normally, I am quite accustomed to seeing grown men wearing shorts and sandals and sleeveless shirts to work, despite their pale skin and flabby muscles. A movie set is filled with such men, and under normal circumstances I would never have blinked an eye.

But the snow, brief though it was, made me take a second look at Cyrus Waggoner. Cyrus generally wore a scraggly little ponytail that peeked out from the adjustable strap at the back of his baseball cap, a Hawaiian print shirt with the sleeves shredded off, and ragged surfer shorts. The total "look" ended at his ankles, however. His job as a member of the lighting crew meant that he needed shoes that kept the state of his toes a secret. His steel-tipped boots protected him as he climbed through the rafters hanging and adjusting the huge, heavy lights required to turn an indoor set into a tropical paradise, and he couldn't risk adding the flip-flops that would have finished his attempt to pass as a genuine beach bum.

Until this moment, I had never given anyone on the lighting crew a second glance. I had taken Cyrus and all his scruffy-but-solidly-shod fellows for granted. I knew he was important to the making of *Soul Responsibility*, the ill-starred, unlucky turkey of a movie on which we had all been toiling for the last several weeks. His job complemented the work of those three guys on electrics who made the props department sing and the wardrobe team function and the set hum and the magic happen. But he had just been one of the masses until the moment he got snowed on.

As the loyal and much-maligned assistant to the film's principal producer, I was only a small cog in the complex Rube Goldberg machine that was our production crew. If you removed me, the marble would still roll down the chute, the dominoes would still fall, the match would still be struck, and the steam kettle would still reach a rolling boil. But if you made Cyrus climb down from his catwalk, the spring at the very end of the track might never be sprung, and that could threaten the future of motion pictures as we know them.

However, he should not have been outside, able to collect snow on the tips of his boots. He should have been inside the soundstage, with the dead body.

For there had also been a corpse on the set that day. Its

presence had upset Dave, the production manager, not because it was dead, but because it interrupted his carefully constructed shooting schedule. It required us all to stop working. A police officer (a real one, not someone in a costume) said so. Dave had shoved his bony little face right up into the officer's and argued for a solid three minutes before it became quite clear that no, a movie production was not more important than the progress of justice and the law. And yes, Dave would have to shut down flming for a couple of expensive hours in order to give the real police the opportunity to take names, dust for fingerprints, compile a police report, and remove the corpse from the middle of Soundstage 26.

Interestingly, Dave didn't seem especially upset about the corpse's identity. You might think he would have been disturbed when the film's most important producer turned up stiff as a board in the middle of the soundstage floor. And this particular producer had once been Mrs. Dave. But the corpse's ex-husband was far more worried about staying on time and on budget. He had other producers to answer to, and a more recent wife to soothe his fevered brow, and he didn't appear to care in any way that was apparent that it was Louisa Davenport who was dead.

Louisa had been a brilliant producer, able to sweet talk the most cautious potential funder out of his life savings, the most difficult star into tackling a possibly-career-ending role, and the most skittish studio executive into a development deal to end all development deals. I had sat at her elbow through more than one business lunch, and I had observed firsthand how she had turned her professional portfolio to gold in even the shakiest markets and her little black book into a Who's Who of Hollywood conquests. I had personally inhaled the heady perfume of her take-no-prisoners methodology. I had taken exhaustive notes and nearly completed my Master's degree at her feet. I had become sure I would have been able to step into her very large footsteps, had she ever been generous enough to give me the slightest opportunity.

But now she was dead, her neck broken and her twisted body lying smack in the middle of the main set of her latest movie. While there had been times I would have liked to have pushed her off a catwalk myself, the timing seemed less than auspicious for my career ambitions. I had been about to ask her for a promotion, but now my future in the business might well have been dashed to the concrete floor along with her brains.

I stared at the toes of Cyrus's boots and wondered who would have benefited from messing with my personal timetable. Dave, of course, had been married to her once. Steve walked her dogs. Johannes was in the middle of supervising construction on an addition to her twenty-three room Bel Air "cottage." Ellis, Marko, and the little guy in accounting whose name I never remembered were always running back and forth to her house with little "deliveries," the nature of which was the cause of much speculation. Declan had been caught kissing her in the darkest corner of the Viper

Room, and it wasn't the kind of kissing you see every day on the streets of Los Angeles. And those were just the first names that came to mind.

Cyrus, however, had no connection to Louisa beyond his employment as one of the grips who crawled around the rafters of soundstages where she was producing things. The fact that he had been outside the door, letting the unusual snow pile up on his boots when Louisa's cold and lifeless corpse had turned up inside should not, in and of itself, had convicted him of any crime.

It might have gotten him fired, though. I know that casual observation of a movie set makes it look as though nobody is doing anything, but everyone there actually has a very specific job, and Cyrus's very specific job had required him to be inside and high up on a catwalk, not hanging out in the fresh air getting snowed on, at least not until somebody had told him it was okay to come down from there.

Yet here he was, pacing outside the soundstage door where one of the production's golf carts usually parked. And suddenly, I thought I knew why.

"Hey, Cyrus," I called, and he halted, confusion in his eyes.

"Didn't know you knew my name," he muttered. He didn't try to run away, but he also didn't move toward me. He simply stood there, a lumpen mass, dripping guilt.

"Of course I know your name, Mr. Waggoner," I

drawled, walking slowly toward him with a smile. "The question is, do you know mine?"

"Um," he replied, and I marveled at his eloquence.

"Not that it matters, but I'm Janet Dial." I stuck out my hand. He looked at it, trying to decide the price of connection. At last, he shook it, though it was just a quick, cautious pump, and he promptly dropped it again, poised to run in case all I really wanted to know was the time.

"Helluva a day, huh?" I asked.

He nodded once. "You work for her." I could see the effort it had taken him to figure out who I was.

"'Worked,'" I corrected. "I did work for her. Guess I need to polish up my resume now, though."

"Huh."

"You worked for her, too," I reminded him. "But I don't believe you need to worry about your job. The show must go on and all that, right?"

He frowned at me, clearly trying to parse whatever meaning he could from my words, and clearly failing.

I smiled at him again. I decided to test my theory. "Is the coffee here any good?" I asked.

He relaxed slightly. This a question he could handle. "Dunno. I stay away from craft services."

"Ah. Trying to keep that girlish figure?"

The frown returned.

"Do you have a cigarette?" I asked, hoping I wouldn't have to take up smoking again just to satisfy my curiosity.

He shook his head. "Don't smoke." He actually looked proud of himself for this.

"So we're on break now until the police finish up," I told him. "But I'm guessing Dave will have us back up and running the second they let him. Schedules to keep and all. I'm sure your boss is feeling the heat." I flipped through my mental Rolodex. "Marko, right? He's your department head?"

His eyes widened for a moment and then flickered away, glancing toward the door into the soundstage. It was all the confirmation I needed. I placed a reassuring hand on his arm, and he flinched as though I had struck him. I took the leap of faith.

"It's okay, Cyrus," I said softly. "You didn't know why Marko spent so much time at her house. You weren't part of that little supply chain, were you?"

His eyes swiveled back to meet mine, and now they were positively enormous. His mouth, however, remained firmly shut, though that in itself was telling. He should have been denying everything or asking what the hell I was talking about or working out a major lie or something. Instead, he was staring at me in abject terror, almost pleading with me to stay as silent as he was.

If he had known me, he would have realized the futility

of that plea.

"You won't get in trouble, not for just being a lookout," I continued, my voice still quiet. "You didn't help him with anything up at the house, did you? You didn't bring Ms. Davenport any of those 'special packages,' right? I never saw you at her back door. I think today was a one-time favor to your boss. You won't lose your job over it, and neither will Marko. The police shouldn't be able to tell that he set up today's little staged scene to cover the fact that he was in a lot deeper than he ever intended to be and finally found a way out. I'm guessing that the autopsy will suggest that she broke her neck by accident, not that she had help meeting her maker."

Cyrus swallowed. I watched the lump in his throat try to make its way past his enormous Adams apple. I took another guess.

"And if they don't make that connection, I'll bet they'll never be able to figure out whatever it is that Marko has on you that got him to convince you to guard this door while he arranged that little scenario inside."

Cyrus was shaking now, but he stayed silent, letting his eyes speak for him as they begged me to keep his secret.

"Don't worry," I said soothingly. "I won't give you away. I don't especially care what Marko did to get you to make sure nobody interrupted him."

I watched him think about that, and I saw the moment

when he started to believe me. His muscles relaxed. His eyes began to return to their normal squint. His breathing calmed.

I waited another moment. "I'll find out, though," I whispered, and I saw all the tension and caution flood back. "You owe me, Cyrus. And so does Marko. And when I produce my first movie, I may have to call in that little debt."

I smiled again. Maybe the timing on Louisa's death hadn't been so bad after all. Maybe the winter snow meant my luck was about to change for good.

IN THE

PUBLIC EYE

by

Mark Hague

YES, LOS ANGELES is car-culture country. But I don't have my own wheels. I rely on public transportation. In Los Angeles that means Metro. I live in Long Beach, a part of the vast Los Angeles megalopolis tucked away in a southern corner of the county. I take buses, as well as the light rail train known as the Blue Line, which travels between Long Beach and L.A. every ten minutes, bringing passengers through the suburban Dominguez Hills, Compton, Willowbrook, Watts, Florence, and the Vernon corridor.

That Friday, I was sitting there idly, looking out the window, numbly watching the sprawl pass by, no actual destination in mind. I was unemployed, and spent my time riding the rails—so to speak. I often took the train between downtowns, Long Beach to Los Angeles, then rode buses from Downtown L.A. into the surrounding cities and communities. I liked to think I was exploring, but I was really just existing between unemployment checks. Thank God for a regional bus pass. I could spend my days going anywhere the participating bus systems allowed without paying one cent more.

I liked the idea of getting off the bus and exploring strange neighborhoods, so I always allotted a large part of my day to roaming. It was early that day, not much past dawn, and the train was crowded with commuters. We'd left behind the Watts Towers, the 103rd Street Station, and come to Firestone

Station in the unincorporated community of Florence. I always had a book to read, but that morning, my attention had flagged. As we came into the station, an elevated platform over Firestone Boulevard, I could see across an empty paved lot and an alley, into the adjoining backyards. The doors opened, people disembarked, and I caught sight of a man digging in his backyard about a block away. The yard was barren—no plants, just dead, sparse grass interspersed with patches of dirt. I only had time to notice the elongated, tarp-wrapped bundle next to the hole he had dug. Obviously, the guy was no gardener, not a regular putterer in his backyard, so why was he digging a hole there? And what was in the bundle? Just then, the train doors closed and the train pulled away, bound for downtown L.A.

I glanced around at my fellow passengers, but no one seemed to have noticed. They either had their eyes closed, were absorbed in their reading, or were simply vegetating. Some women were putting on make-up. And I realized that had I been in the next car or even in a different seat a few rows up from where I was, I wouldn't have seen anything either.

On impulse, I got off at the next station—Florence— and took the train back to Firestone. When I glanced down from the platform the man was still digging, so I got off the train and took the stairs down to street level. Usually I'm pretty good at orienting myself and figuring out which direction I need to go. But I was a little turned around, so it took a moment to decide which alley I'd need to take to get closer to that backyard. I trekked along until I reached a chain link fence separating the alley from the backyard of the house. I positioned myself in a spot where I was hidden and watched the man throw his shovel down, stoop and then laboriously pull the tarp-covered bundle into the hole. I watched him fill in the hole, all the while looking around, as if to make sure no one was noticing him.

He hadn't seen me. And I was hidden far enough away that I wasn't obvious, but a chill settled over me, even in the warm Los Angeles winter. Careful to make sure I wasn't seen, I hurried back to the train station to continue my journey downtown.

For the rest of the day, I couldn't stop thinking about the scene I'd witnessed. What had he been burying back there? I kept mentally going back to the scene time and again, all through my trip out to the Glendale Galleria on the Short Bus 63, while wandering the mall for a couple of hours of people watching, and while traveling along Route 95 back to downtown L.A. Eventually I caught the train back to Long Beach. And, yes, I did pay particular attention to that faded white stucco house with its back wall covered in black graffiti. But since I'd slightly misjudged the seating, I couldn't see the yard until the train was leaving the station. I caught only a fleeting glimpse of it as the train picked up speed. Of course, the man was long gone and while I thought I could see the slightly mounded spot where the object was buried, I doubted anyone else would have noticed.

That night, online, I read about a coed who'd gone missing from USC the night before. My mind immediately went to the tarp-wrapped bundle. No, it couldn't be. The house wasn't close enough to campus. Besides, people disappeared all the time, right? Hardly a day went by in Los Angeles without someone being reported missing. And people dig holes for other reasons than burying bodies. No, it was just a coincidence. Wasn't it? All the same, I found it very hard to get to sleep that night.

❉   ❉   ❉

THE NEXT DAY I got up early and took the Blue Line back to the Firestone Station. I kept asking myself what the hell I was doing. It wasn't my concern what the man had been doing in his own backyard. And yet I couldn't stop thinking about what I had seen. I couldn't stop thinking about that poor girl. I passed the neighborhood bar midway down the block, its stucco walls imbued with long decades of stale beer fumes, cigarette smoke and desperation. I walked past the alley entrance, and tried to find the front of the house on the next street, counting the number of houses until I was sure I had the right one. At least it was coated in the same off-white stucco, and there was a faded brick-red house next door, just like I had noticed in the back the day before. There was just a short chain-link fence separating the house from the street and from its two neighbors. The front yard was made up of

21

cracked cement squares, and was as bare as the back, the dead grass bedraggled and succumbing to the dirt beneath it, in contrast to the lush bushes in the neighboring yards to either side.

Spying a battered metal mailbox on a post next to the gate, I was struck with an idea. I looked around quickly. Seeing no one on the street, I opened the box with trembling fingers. There was only one envelope inside. It was addressed to the electric company, but it had the name Roger Wilcoxson above the return address of the house. My heart pounding, I returned the envelope to the mailbox.

A flash of curtain in the window caught my eye. I looked up. I gasped as I saw the man from the other day scowling at me from the other side of the window. At least it looked like him: a small, mousy, brown-haired man with the same build and...was it dirt under his fingernails? He disappeared and I walked hurriedly away, not wanting any confrontation.

I heard the front door open behind me. Someone yelled "Hey!" but I was already pretty far down the street. When I looked back, he wasn't pursuing me. My heart still beating hard in my chest, I ran back to the train station. That was it, I thought, I wasn't interested really in why any Roger Wilcoxson would want to dig a hole in his backyard. Not my business, not my worry. I'd spent too much time reading mystery novels—fiction!—and had let my imagination get the better of me.

I took the Blue Line to the terminus in downtown Los Angeles, and then took the Red Line out to the Universal City Station, where I boarded the Orange Line bus to Warner Center. I wandered around the mall there for a while, finally treating myself to my favorite coffee ice cream with chocolate chips and cinnamon. Eventually, the panic of the morning having faded, I emerged from the air conditioned mall and started my journey back to Long Beach.

It was over. Roger Wilcoxson might have seen me, but he didn't know who I was. Maybe he was a murderer, maybe not. Either way, it was none of my business. And even if he wanted to make it my business now, there was no way he could find me. So why did I Google the man's name that evening at home? Or the address? Why did I read article after article about that poor missing girl? I was able to identify Wilcoxson as the owner of the house, but other than this, I couldn't find much about the man himself, or connect him to the student's disappearance.

And yet I couldn't leave it alone. I thought about it all weekend, and on Monday, I found myself out by Firestone Boulevard again, watching Roger Wilcoxson leave his house. Dressed in a white shirt and black pants this time, he walked down the street toward Firestone Station.

This was madness. I had spent too much time on this. Resolving one last time to let it go, I pulled out my cell phone and called the police. I reported what I'd seen, gave the address, the owner's name, and even a brief description of the house. Figuring I'd done all I could do, I went on my way. I took the number two bus out to Malibu that day, walked along the beach and then back, determined not to give Roger Wilcoxson another thought.

❀   ❀   ❀

A COUPLE OF days later, I was talking with a neighbor who worked for the local police department. I explained to him what I'd seen and reported. He laughed. Was I aware of how many crank calls just like that the police received in a day? No judge would allow a warrant to search the man's premises on such flimsy evidence. "Give it up," he suggested. "Go back to your mystery books."

But I couldn't. Knowing I might be that young woman's only chance for justice, I couldn't leave it alone.

❀   ❀   ❀

ON WEDNESDAY I went out and bought a shovel, and on Friday, a week to the day that I had seen Roger Wilcoxson bury something in his backyard, I took the Blue Line back out to Firestone. I had taken pains to wrap the shovel up so it didn't look like a shovel, but I probably shouldn't have bothered—I was in L.A., after all, and people carried around all sorts of strange things. Still, I didn't want to attract any attention. I positioned myself down the street from the front of the Wilcoxson house and prepared to wait for him to leave that morning. But the curtains were open, and the house was deserted. Tamping down a sense of panic, I approached his house, putting the shovel down on the sidewalk in front of the thick bushes next door, and went up to ring his doorbell. When there was no answer, I knocked. There was still no answer, so I retrieved the shovel and went around to the back of the house. I climbed over the chain link fence into the yard. I felt awfully exposed. I knew I was trespassing. I looked around to see if anyone had noticed, but saw no one. Then I heard the train passing and realized, with some little consternation, that someone might be seeing me in that yard from the train—just as I had seen Wilcocxson a week before. They might be wondering what I was doing. But there was no time to worry about that now.

I found the spot where he had been digging. There were other areas that looked like they had been dug at various times as well. I put the blade of the shovel into the ground and dug. It wasn't difficult as the soil was still loose from Wilcoxson's excavation a week before. It wasn't long before I uncovered the edge of the tarp. I knelt and tore the plastic.

"Shit!"

A hand dropped out, its grey, nasty, nails still painted red. I sprang up and scrambled over the fence and down the alley, where I puked. Was it the missing USC student? Did it matter? Wilcoxson had a body—probably more than one— buried in his back yard! I had to make the police come to the house. But how, considering they probably thought I was a crank? Not to mention that I had illegally dug up someone else's back yard. I looked around. How could I get the authorities' attention?

I saw a trash barrel behind one of the neighboring houses. I pulled it over to the yard and lit the paper inside. I called 911 and reported a fire in the back yard, giving Wilcoxson's address. Then I climbed back over the fence.

In no time, I was back up on the train platform with my shovel, hoping the fire engine would pull up before the fire was out. I figured that the firefighters would discover the body while putting out the fire, and that they would alert the police, if there wasn't already an officer accompanying the fire truck. It wasn't long before the fire engine came, accompanied by a black and white. I let out a sigh of relief as I boarded the train to Long Beach. I'd done all I could do.

Even as early as it still was, I was exhausted, and I just wanted to go home.

Before the train pulled out, I saw the firefighters and the uniformed police officer peer into the hole, pointing and gesticulating. Obviously they had seen the tarp and the grisly thing that had spilled out of it.

Giddy with relief, I grinned as the train pulled out of the station. I took out my book, habitually glancing around at my fellow passengers.

Suddenly my breath caught, and my stomach clenched. In the corner seat, scowling at me, but with a smirk, was Roger Wilcoxson.

BURNT

DECEMBER

by

Lee Mullins

CHAPTER 1

"I DON' WANNA GO!"

"And why don't you want to go, Your Majesty?"

"Cuz Stanley be hittin' me all the time."

Stanley could be most accurately described as my daughter Anastasia's best friend and worst enemy. She likes her friends sharp and funny. Problem was, Stanley was also a bully. Most of the time he only bullied other kids at the preschool, but lately he'd taken to hitting Tasia, and she was having none of it.

"He wasn't at school yesterday, maybe he won't be there again today," I told her in my best reasonable dad voice, desperate to drop her off so I wouldn't be late for work at the coroner's office. I firmly walked my daughter up the steps and into St. Alfred's, also known as St. Alfred the not-so-Great's, Preschool and Enrichment Center. We said hello to the stream of people coming down the stairs, including Deacon Smith from the church and a bunch of mothers and fathers who had already dropped their kids off.

When we got to the classroom, Tasia asked the ever-cheerful Miss Tonya about Stanley. Miss Tonya said his momma had called in to say he had the flu and would be out for a couple of days. So Her Majesty agreed to stay. I had no premonition then of what was about to befall us all. We just walked to her cubicle to drop her stuff and I helped her get out of her full winter princess gear, including pink jacket, pink boots and pink glitter mittens. We said "hi" to Miss Elma, Miss Tonya's co-teacher, who was preparing the morning snack, and to Mr. Trevor the music teacher. Miss Elma was a solidly built woman with a huge Supremes-style beehive hairdo. She nodded curtly at us. I always wondered why she worked as a teacher, as she had no love of humanity.

Mr. Trevor, on the other hand, was a friend to everyone. He was also St. Alfred's usual Santa Claus — even if he was a bit thin and sickly for the job — and general handyman. That morning, he was trying to fix yet another hole in the wall. St. Alfred's drywall and small children were not a great combination. He stopped long enough to try to give Tasia a hug hello. Tasia was having none of that, either. "I don't like him hugging me," she said loud enough that I hoped he hadn't heard her, and walked quickly away to her morning circle. I grinned ruefully before wishing Mr. Trevor a good day. I briefly joined Tasia in the circle, kissed her goodbye, and then walked out into the cold December morning to face death once again.

I'm a first year medical student at Temple University here in Philadelphia. As I got a child and a wife I need to support, I also work two outside jobs, one at the mortuary my Aunt Yvonne runs with her husband Albert. Never known my dad, and my mom moved down to North Carolina to help my Uncle Henry, her and Yvonne's older brother, with his diner. Yvonne, Albert and their family are all the extended family I got around here. My other job is out in the 'burbs at the East Chester Medical Examiner's Office.

I'm a med student because I want to use science to help people, but I scare small children and adults alike. Something about being a 6′5 black guy with a claw for a right hand freaks people out. I was born with just an extra big forefinger and a thumb. Fine for writing and cutting, but I can't play basketball for shit. I've come to peace with this and am going into pathology. Since I've been working at Aunt Yvonne and Uncle Bert's mortuary since I was a kid, I've also developed a fondness for dead people. Never seen a dead person turn away from me, give me back talk, or insist upon telling me their business. You gotta ask a dead person in just the right way to get any answers at all outta them. Course the same can't be said of the people you work with in this business.

❊   ❊   ❊

"Welcome to Motel Deep 6," trilled Elvis as I entered the office. How a short, blond, totally gay guy who must sing tenor came to be named after The King I do not know. I thought I knew a lotta words for dead people, but Elvis has me beat by a mile. "Old Man is looking at a French Fry in Room 2.

Smoking in bed at some fleabag palace."

"Ah, yes," I responded in my best Sherlock Holmes voice, "a habitué of the third floor hell that is the smoking section of the Super Budget Inn." Elvis didn't immediately tell me I was full of bovine excrement, so I was obviously right. My wife Emilee is a student in anthropology and also works as a hotel clerk. She had told me this morning when she came in that there had been a fire at the Super Budget. Tales of the fire had spread fast through the night clerk network. Never met a bigger bunch of gossips than hotel night clerks. Almost nothing ever happens at 2:00 a.m. so the merest hint of smoke becomes news broadcast to 150 local area night staff.

"Old Man thinks it is an open and shut case," continued Elvis. "Antoine Jones, medium height, 47 years old, very thin guy, checked in at 10pm. Three alarm fire by 1 a.m. Toasted fish stick retrieved at 3 a.m. Not much to see but his ex-wife identified a watch and what was left of his shoes that the boys found after the fire." "The boys" was Elvis's generic term for the members of East Chester police department even though they were as likely to be cynical 60 year old ladies as eager young men.

Old Man, a.k.a. Seymour Higgenbothum, my boss and East Chester Coroner, came blasting out of Room 2. His basic life theory was the faster he did things, the more money he would save the taxpayers of East Chester. "Death by incineration. Victim drinking and smoking in bed. Went up like a match stick." He noticed me some time during this pronouncement. "Claw, drop the body at your uncle's when you get off work."

"Sure," I replied, gritting my teeth at him calling me Claw. I know this is what everyone has called me as long as I can remember, but I prefer the name from people I actually like. From him, I want Mr. Harrington or at least Charles. Having me transport bodies in my off-hours in my 1992 Toyota van kept the gas costs down for the hearse and was another way to save money for the taxpayers of East Chester. That hearse guzzled gas like nobody's business, according to him. My theory is that he was skimming some off for his retirement fund.

"Let me assist you with Mr. Matchstick," said Elvis. "It's cold enough outside that he'll keep fine until you go home." I nodded and we scooped up the charred body and sundry bags of organs on the examining table, deposited them in one of our generic coffins, and wheeled him to the chilly back of the Toyota. Elvis usually works night shifts but is good about staying around long enough to do anything easier done with two people. He then checked out for the day with an "Arrivederci, Dr. Zhivago!"

The rest of the day was quiet. Only one old man came in. He had died at home of a heart attack and was found by his cleaning lady almost a week later. Stunk up the office for a while, but Lysol IC and running the fans for an hour solved that. Otherwise all was quiet in the grand metropolis of Brookville, East Chester County, the smallest and most corrupt of the Philadelphia area suburbs. It gives West Chester a good name.

❊   ❊   ❊

I LEFT WHEN Tom Smith—the Zombie, as Elvis usually calls him—arrived for the evening shift. I then headed back to West Philly to St. Alfred's to pick up Tasia. She's gotten used to driving around with dead bodies. Better riding around with a corpse in the back seat than risking the ire of Miss Elma, who got really cranky by the end of the day. I expected just to shoot in, grab Tasia and all her royal pink garb, and head over to Aunt Yvonne's, where we usually spent our Tuesday nights, as Emilee had class. But all hell was breaking loose at St. Alfred's.

"Where's Stanley?" a woman was screaming. "What's that bitch of an ex-daughter-in-law done with my grandson?"

"She called this morning to say that he has the flu and will be out for a couple of days," said Miss Elma, just short of screaming herself. Miss Tonya was nowhere to be seen, so Miss Elma was having to deal with everything by herself.

"She hates when he's sick," yelled the woman, "She always sticks him with me when he's got even a cold. Somebody gimme a phone!"

I handed her my cell and she punched some numbers. "You got Stanley?" she asked angrily. The voice on the other side said something. The woman, obviously Stanley's grandmother, started yelling again. "She said she got a call from school saying I was picking up Stanley for the weekend. I never take him weekends. I have better things to do than deal with that little bastard on weekends. What have you done with him?"

Tasia started crying. "What happened to Stanley? Where's Stanley? What did you do to my friend?"

Miss Elma took the phone. "Who called you? What did they say?" Somebody had called and left a message on her voice mail that Mrs. Wilson had arranged to pick up Stanley after school on Friday to visit family in Delaware. Stanley's mother hadn't been worried because, as Miss Elma said she said, "It was just like that old bag to take Stanley down to her relatives without talkin' to me about it first."

"You've kidnapped Stanley!" yelled Mrs. Wilson.

Miss Elma lost it. "Why the hell would we want Stanley? We can't wait to get rid of him by the end of the day!"

"What did you do to Stanley?" cried Tasia again, probably the only one of all of us that actually liked Stanley at least some of the time.

"I'm calling the cops," said Miss Elma.

Mrs. Wilson hesitated.

"I'll call my brother. He's with Philly PD," said Miss Elma. "He can ask some questions."

"I went to school with Terrence Jackson," I added, knowing exactly who Miss Elma was going to call. "He's a good guy."

Mrs. Wilson nodded slowly. "Never liked the po-lice, but I guess we have to."

Tasia seemed calmer at this information as well, so I made my move. "Come on honey, we don't want to be late for Aunt Yvonne's dinner." And, I thought to myself, I needed to get that burnt corpsicle outta my van. We left just as Terrence pulled up in the same old Chevy he'd been driving since high school. We exchanged quick a "Wha's up?" but no more as we each headed to do our business. Reminded me that I needed to call him to say "hi" sometime.

CHAPTER 2

I FINALLY GOT to the funeral home, marked by its ever-familiar "Jordan Mortuary, Bringing Families Peace Since 1957" sign. I kissed Yvonne hello, dropped Tasia with her cousins Dynillia and Tyrone, and headed to the back. "Got a burn victim in the van," I told my aunt.

"We got a call," said Yvonne. "Bert's waiting for you in the back." I nodded and went to drive the van back to the loading dock. Bert and I got the coffin out without any trouble. There was really nothing left to Mr. Matchstick, just a couple of organs and a crispy shell smelling like sausage as burn victims usually do.

"Mr. Jones's ex-wife called," said Bert. "Said the service will be at St. Alfred's on Saturday. Said to see if we could do an open casket but would understand if we couldn't."

"He's pretty toasted. Would be a lotta work to do the whole body. Maybe we could do something with his head and shoulders if we got some decent photos. Not much left of the rest of him."

Bert and I lifted him onto the table. "Huh," said Bert after he briefly looked over the shriveled body with Higgenbothum's sloppy orange coroner's stitches across the head and chest. "Musta married young to have an ex-wife already." I followed his eyes to the bones of the legs visible through what was left of his charred skin. There was no fusion of the epiphysis, no caps on the long bones.

"According to Higgenbothum, he was a 47-year-old male, but this guy can't be more than 15," I said, after looking at the bones more closely.

"Jesus," muttered my uncle. "Another East Chester mess exported to West Philly." He looked at me. "Do you trust Higgenbothum to fix things?"

"Nope," I replied. "He's an ass. But I got friend there that might be able to help out."

"Call 'em," said Bert. "I don't like unidentified customers."

I grabbed my phone and called. "Hey Elvis, it's Claw. Got a problem. I'm at Jordan Mortuary, and that 47-year-old the old man identified is probably about 15."

"How delicious!" exclaimed Elvis. "I do so love a mystery."

I had to laugh, but did manage to say, "My uncle doesn't. Why don't you come and take a look?"

"Be there in a twinkle," he said and hung up.

Aunt Yvonne came down stairs. "You boys ready for dinner yet? I got a casserole waiting."

"Nothing we can do here right now," replied Bert going to wash his hands. "Coroner says this brother is a 47-year-old but he sent us a 15-year-old. Claw's got a friend coming over from East Chester that is gonna take a look."

Yvonne nodded and walked back to the front of the

house. I followed when my hands were clean as well.

"Who's he supposed to be?" she asked as I went to the kitchen.

"Antoine Jones."

"Low life," replied Yvonne. "Was glad when Sadie kicked him out of the house."

The casserole and kids interrupted the rest of the conversation. Tasia has a big crush on her cousin Tyrone so the trick at family dinners is to stop her from egging him on to more and more outrageous actions. Aunt Yvonne moved Tyrone's juice out of the way so he didn't hit it as he was telling a story about school and I removed a bread stick Tasia was waving around in her hand. After we saved the world from the dangers of a moving feast, we settled down the kids with books and homework and the promise of TV when they finished and went back again to see our young friend.

Elvis showed up just as we were gloving up. He had the digital video camera from the lab. "Let's do this right," he said. "You do a formal autopsy, and I'll record it. And then you can film me as I do one as well. Given the Old Man already missed stuff, I think that the more eyes we can get on this the better."

I looked at my Uncle Bert. "You lead this," he said. "You know what you need to say to the dang machine. Me and Yvonne will chip in when we see something."

I had never done an autopsy myself before but I had watched enough to know the format. I ran through examination type, place, presentation, postmortem changes as best as I could and we all contributed to identification.

"Originally identified from driver's license and motel video camera as Antoine Jones, 47 year old African American male. Now John Doe, approximately 14-16 year old African American male, 120-140 pounds, 5'6 to 5'8, short dark hair. Body presents developed and extensive 3rd degree burns over almost 95% of body including face."

We went through the body systematically from top to bottom. Yvonne, who does all our reconstructions, pointed out that his face completely different from Jones'.

"Antoine was from Oklahoma, had those high Scotty Pippin cheekbones. This kid is pure Philadelphia," she said after lightly running her gloved hand over the black crumpled face in front of us.

The teeth looked like a 50-year-old man's, falling apart from cavities and yellow from smoking. The arms and legs were twisted up in classic burn victim fetal position. Bert then discussed the lack of fusion of the epiphysis. We also found slight signs of rickets. So no sun or milk in the kid's life. After we finished the head to toe examination, we went through the organs that had been packed in two baggies at his feet, taking samples from the stomach and other tissues for further testing. Lungs showed inhalation of smoke and carbon deposits in the trachea.

We all dealt with death. We were morticians and coroners. But each sign of the burning caused us to wince. This wasn't a drunken guy that had smoked in bed. This was a kid deliberately burned to death. After I finished, Elvis started to repeat the examination. First thing he said was, "Such a thin kid for all that junk food he ate." He looked up at Albert and me. "Did Higgenbothum do an AIDS test?"

Albert shrugged and I shook my head. "Not that I know of," I replied.

"Been doing some outreach so have a couple of OraQuicks in the car," said Elvis, "Lemme grab one. Not ideal but better than waiting for tomorrow." He left and came back quickly. I held open the kid's mouth as best as I could and Elvis took a sample of what was left of his saliva. "We can use blood if this doesn't work for some reason," Elvis said as he set the test stick on a counter out of the way. He then came back and confirmed everything that I had found, the cavities, the rickets, the sunless conditions the kid must have been held in. Afterwards, he went back to check the test.

I've seen OraQuick tests before. The top red line on stick usually shows up quickly and clearly, confirming that the test has been done correctly. It is the bottom line that you have to worry about. Even if someone is HIV+, it is often faint. Not this one. It glared bright, dark red.

"Jesus help us," murmured someone, probably Yvonne.

I managed to not throw up, but just barely.

When we finally could turn the camera off, there was a stunned silence. I summed up our findings. "We have the body of a young man who has AIDS, probably kept out of sight of the sun, and lived on nothing but soda and cigarettes." Everyone responded after that.

I heard "Fucked up," from Elvis.

"No life for a child," said Yvonne.

Bert was the one who said the most obvious thing. "We need to call the cops now."

I picked up my phone. "I'll call Terrence Jackson, he's a detective these days." Everyone agreed. Not the conversation I'd wanted to have with Terrence but had to be done.

"Hey, Terrence, it's Claw," I said after I got a hold of him. "We got a body here originally identified as 47 year old Antoine Jones by Higgenbothum over in East Chester but is probably only 15 years old. We think it's murder."

Terrence was never real chatty, just said, "Where you at?" and "Be right there." We cleaned up and went to wait in the front parlor.

CHAPTER 3

YVONNE POURED TERRENCE a cup of coffee and fed him a piece of her fine banana bread and we began to review our autopsy results. He too was brought up short by Elvis's description of the body.

"You think he was a runaway turning tricks?" Terrence asked.

Elvis shrugged. "Maybe. Some street kids'll start turning tricks at eleven or twelve. But if the OraQuick was right, his viral load is way high for someone with a recent HIV infection. I'm no expert but it looks like it could be a decade of abuse to me."

Terrence just shook his head. We had nothing to add to the conversation so just waited for him to say something. He finally said, "Let me start by seeing the body and the autopsy tape." After he had had a look at John Doe and the tape, we went back to the parlor. "Well," said Terrence. "We got a guy who ain't dead, and some poor kid who is. Claw, can you issue a death certificate?"

"I can't," I said, "But Elvis can. He's an official assistant coroner."

Terrence nodded and asked Elvis, "Would you feel comfortable issuing a death certificate for our John Doe?"

"Glad to issue a second certificate," replied Elvis. "I have forms in my car."

"I suggest what we do is to report the murder of John Doe, but let the proceedings for Mr. Jones proceed as normal," continued Terrence. "He is involved in this somehow and his funeral is the best shot we have at seeing who is interested in his death. Who's paying for his funeral?"

"Ex-wife, Sadie Jones," said Bert. "She mentioned something about insurance money."

"You might never get paid for this one," replied Terrence.

Yvonne and Bert glanced at each other and Yvonne nodded slightly. She kept the books. "Payment would be welcome but if a good send-off will help catch the creep who did this, we are happy to help whatever happens," answered Bert. Then his business side reasserted himself. "Maybe we can do a memorial fund once we figure out who this poor kid is."

"Can you make him look like Jones?" asked Terrence.

Bert smiled. "My lovely wife is the Michelangela of mortician's wax. She could reconstruct you to look like Dolly Parton if she felt like it."

"Ooh what fun!" declared Elvis. "You would look fabulous in a blonde bouffant."

Terrence growled in reply.

"I can even remove the wax afterwards," said Yvonne, moving the conversation away from so obviously dangerous waters, "So we can give the poor child back a more appropriate face at some later point."

"By any chance could you make a sketch or a bust of what he would have actually looked like?" asked Terrence. "The department can pay you for that at least."

"Happy to try," replied Yvonne.

"And it'll give us a start when looking for our missing person," said Terrence. "Not much to go on, right now. You know they never spend the big bucks on finding the murderer of an unidentified black kid in West Philly who was actually killed in East Chester."

Elvis seemed to be ready to say something and then hesitated for a second. "Not that I think that the piece of rancid barracuda that did this is actual a part of the active and open Philadelphia gay community," he eventually said, "But somebody might have a lead or two on a perpetrator who is HIV+ if asked correctly." He beamed. "And Gay Bingo is this week, biggest AIDS fundraiser in Philly! I will be a BVD and would be delighted to score you some tickets even though we have been sold out for weeks!"

I of course have heard of Gay Bingo, as has any public radio listener in Philly. But I had not twigged that Elvis would be involved. My gaydar commonsense is completely lacking. "You are a roller skating Bingo Verifying Diva?" I managed to squeak out.

"But of course!" declared Elvis. "I am Elvirus, the Queen, the blonde diva of your dreams!"

Terrence rolled his eyes.

"Always wanted to go," said Yvonne, "Just the place

for my red sequined dress."

"I'll watch the kids," responded Bert.

I grinned. "Good, I'll leave Tasia with you as well. It is as close to a date as I will get with Emilee for a long time. I can't wait to see this."

We all looked at Terrence. "Okay, okay, I'll come too," he said.

"Not a lot of people come from West Philly," said Elvis, "But I'll make sure you get seats near them."

Terrence had been writing notes all evening and summarized his thoughts. "I'll do a search for a Philadelphia area boys who have gone missing over the last ten years. We'll all meet tomorrow night at Gay Bingo."

"Ooh, it'll be fun!" said Elvis with a grin at Terrence's obvious distaste at these words.

Terrence continued, "And then also at Mr. Jones' funeral...." He looked to Yvonne.

"Next Monday," she replied. "Very simple two-hour viewing here in the morning, a quick service at St. Andrew's in the afternoon. Our weekday budget special."

"That'll work," said Terrence. "Give us time to look at tox reports and any other leads we have."

Elvis nodded, "I'll do these reports tonight and get them to you by tomorrow morning." He glanced down at his watch at this. "Oops, my pumpkin coach to the morgue awaits me, need to bid you good night my lovelies."

Yvonne helped him pack up his tissue samples and he exited with a cheery, "And tomorrow's theme is 'Burlesque and

Buff!' I know you'll do us proud."

"Time for me to go as well," I said. "Maybe Emilee knows something about the Super Budget Inn."

"That'll be good," said Terrence. "Let me know what you find. I can go play flatfoot if you find anything that needs following up."

I agreed. I then went and picked up a sleeping Tasia from the spare bed in Dynillia's room and took us both home.

CHAPTER 4

THE NEXT MORNING did not start well. Tasia woke up early crying. She's been around the funeral home and bodies since she was a babe in arms, and is an old pro at dealing with death, but she must have picked up some of our conversation.

"I don't want Stanley to die like that man," she sobbed.

I comforted her as best as I could, telling her reassuring lies that Stanley was going to be just fine and back bothering her any day now. She went uneasily back to sleep.

Then I got a call from Elvis. He'd run a test for CD-4 cells. John Doe had a cell count of 155 cells/mm3. The kid had had a full blown case of AIDS. My heart sank. I'd dismissed Tasia's worries but suddenly the image of Stanley in the hands of this swine haunted me. I gave a quick run down of Stanley's disappearance to Elvis, agreed with him that attending Gay Bingo was now a necessity, and hung up in order to call Terrence.

"Detective Jackson speaking," he said in a deep rumble. He worked the afternoon and evening shift and I must have just ruined his morning as well.

"Terrence, just got a call from Elvis confirming that John Doe had advanced AIDS." I drew a breath and continued. "And Tasia woke up crying this morning worried that Stanley was going to be killed as well. My gut says she might be right. If it was a child molester that did this and he wanted another random kid to abuse, Stanley has always been a kid at loose ends."

"Crap," Terrence growled. "If that's right though, does bring us back here to West Philly. At least some place to try. I'll call you if I find anything."

"Sounds good, man. I'll be in class all day, just leave a message if you need to," I answered.

"K, later."

Emilee came home from just after I got off the phone. My wife is the most gorgeous woman I've ever seen but she always looks like the cat dragged her in after the night shift. I kissed her good morning, and started scrambling eggs for us all for breakfast. No time to talk really, just told her Tasia had a bad night because she was worried about Stanley going missing. She went to wake her up. Tasia always feels better when her mom is there in the morning.

I put our breakfast on the table, wolfed down mine and headed out for class. Gotta love the joys of Dr. Nevins mumbling about the cardiovascular system. Emilee would drop Tasia off at St. Alfred's and then come back and crash. So much for together time. I hoped she would agree to a night of Gay Bingo. Imagining her in red sequins kept me going the whole day.

Dreams do come true. When I got a hold of her after she woke up and explained that Bert could watch Tasia, she said she'd be happy to go. Anthropologists love ritual so I figured she'd be cool with it. When I got home to change, she was shimmying into one of her prom dresses from high school. It wasn't the red sequins that had kept me going all day, but some kinda dark blue. It looked great on her the first time she wore it and now that she was a little curvier, she looked incredible. Her breasts seemed to be ready to bounce out. What a great night it was shaping up to be. Tasia was in our bedroom helping her dress, suggesting earrings and shoes. I put on the better of my two funeral suits and Tasia helped me pick out the loudest and bluest bowtie possible. We were fired up and ready to go.

We dropped off Tasia with Bert and picked up Yvonne. We met Terrence at the Gresham Y. Terrence grinned when we began to unbutton ourselves from our heavy coats. "Damn Emilee," he said, "You make me remember why I could never love another woman. Never met a girl who could hold a candle to you."

I glowered at him but then my attention was taken away by my aunt. Yvonne had indeed worn her red sequined dress and looked pretty sexy for an old lady. Terrence wore an old skool suit.

"My grandfather bought it after he hit the lottery," he said in his usual gruff voice. "Was a $100 suit in the days that $100 meant something."

As we walked up the stairs to the auditorium, all the elderly drag queens giving out the programs and directing traffic admired the ladies, but Terrence was the one who got the long looks. When we entered the old tall auditorium, it was filled with tables and well-dressed people, mostly white. A blonde in shiny gold and a crown rolled up to us on skates. Took me a minute to figure out that it was Elvis. He was in rare form.

"Ladies, you look spectacular, the belles of the ball," he trilled. "You're making all us divas just greeeeen with envy." However, the real admiration was saved for Terrence. "And Detective Jackson, don't you look fine tonight, a fabulous parcel just wrapped up in pinstripes," said Elvis, stroking his arm. Terrence has trash-talked about 'fags' as long as I have known him but seemed to take this in stride. Probably a good thing as gay bashing wouldn't go down well with this crowd. Way too many gym-toned bodies for the comfort of a skinny dude who spent too many hours in morgues and libraries.

Elvis took us over to a table at the front of the auditorium where an older couple was sitting. She was wearing an enormous purple feather boa. Fit right in with the rest of the crowd. Yvonne of course recognized both of them immediately. "Aunt Mavis! Deacon Smith!" Yvonne introduced all of us to them. Deacon Smith never says much, but nodded hello to all of us. Aunt Mavis, who I think is actually some kind of cousin of my grandmother's, did most of the talking. She told us how tall I was, how pretty the ladies were, but like everyone else, saved the most of her attention for Terrence. "You dress up real nice, young man."

Mavis turned out to be an ex-burlesque dancer and started regaling us with tales of the old days in Vegas and on Broad Street. According her version of history, burlesque and the gay theatre crowd went way back. Every brother and half the older white guys in crowd stopped by to say hi to her and Deacon Smith, so she probably was right about that. The visiting stopped when the lights blinked to announce the show was to begin. The hostess was a red head with great legs, Carlota Ttendant. I am so stupid it took me a moment to remember that she was a drag queen. The show was part Las Vegas, including every bad drag queen joke out there; part gay dating service where all the breeders, meaning the straight people like me and Emilee, sat down, leaving a whole bunch of very attractive gay people standing up; and part sad tributes to people who had died of AIDS. Stanley was a bratty pain in the ass, but did not deserve to be one of the people remembered at Gay Bingo.

Then the games began. We got a bunch of cards and desperately tried to keep up with Carlota as she called numbers. Aunt Mavis was a pro, though. She had 20 cards in front of her and could lay down markers with both hands. Funniest part was when an O-69 was called, you had to stand up, wave your arms and shake your booty. Damn, my wife is sexy when she shakes that fine behind of hers. Terrence looked reluctant until Aunt Mavis told him that if he didn't do it with us, Carlota would make him do it by himself, and she was serious! Elvis just grinned at us as we were all shaking. He also sent round a steady stream of BVDs from Ida Slapter to Ophelia Ballsack. Some were unnervingly attractive, like Ivana Humpdew, while another looked nothing so much like a linebacker from University High School with a wig. We gossiped a little with each, but I couldn't see any connection between any of these rolling divas and the ugly death we were dealing with.

Between visits, I got to talk with Emilee a little bit about the Super Budget Inn. She just said it was pretty typical of the lower end of the motel scale. She agreed to ask around to see whether someone had some information about the fire, but didn't expect to find much. Terrence said he had a couple of leads on who John Doe might be that he was chasing down. Yvonne asked Aunt Mavis a bunch of questions but Mavis didn't know Antoine Jones and only vaguely knew Sadie Jones. She did agree to go to the funeral Monday though. Funerals seemed to be second only to bingo for entertainment in Aunt Mavis's eyes.

And that was really all there was to Gay Bingo. The BVDs skated around every time some yelled "Bingo!" Aunt Mavis made a fair amount of money. I saw more gay guys in one place than I'd ever seen in my life, but we were no further in answering who killed John Doe. And worse, what had happened to Stanley? Even the sight of Emilee's incredible breasts didn't make that much better.

And that was the high point of the week. For the rest of the week there was no news on who John Doe was, no news on Antoine Jones, and no news on Stanley. Uneasy waiting was our lot.

CHAPTER 5

ONLY ANTOINE'S EX-WIFE, Sadie, showed up at the viewing on Monday morning. "I told my family not to bother," she told me between games of solitaire on her iPhone. "Kids don't need to be taken outta school for this bastard." She glanced at the coffin. "Your Aunt Yvonne did a great job, though. He hasn't looked so good since he was 30." Since I had to skip class to be there, I didn't feel guilty about taking out a textbook and catching up on my reading. I just hoped something would happen with the funeral in the afternoon. I left Sadie at 11:00 to head up to school for lab and came back down in time for the funeral itself.

St. Alfred's usually had a pretty good turnout for a funeral, but not a lot of people seemed to care about Antoine Jones. Sadie's family was there, mostly older women and a couple of teenagers too young to be suspects. Some cousins of Antoine's had come down from New York, and there were a few local neighborhood people including Aunt Mavis and Deacon Smith. All of us from Jordan Mortuary were also there. St. Alfred's is a pretty big church, can seat 500 easily, more if people squeeze. There must have been less than 30 people altogether. They all looked kinda lost under the tall ceiling and big old-fashioned stained glass windows.

Aunt Mavis was good at taking up space though. She stood at the entrance to the pew she usually used, greeted everybody and called across the pews to newcomers, occasionally making outrageous comments. When Elvis walked across the back of the church, she said in a whisper that could have been heard across the street, "He's done well for himself, given his terrible family." I had to laugh. Elvis had one of the dullest families ever. He was from Ardmore, where his dad was a dentist and his mother was Ardmore housewife. Mavis had a funny definition of terrible.

Then the organ music started up, and the Reverend Clara Cuthbert entered. She gave a short and not-very-sincere sermon about how Antoine was "a family man taken from us too soon." A couple of songs were sung, the service ended, and people all went to say hello to Sadie. The only nice thing most people could find to say was that Antoine looked great. I realized as I went up to close the coffin with Uncle Bert that I hadn't seen Terrence all day and wondered what had happened to him. He came hustling in just as everyone was leaving.

"I found out who our boy was," he said in a rush. "Sammy Dillon. Disappeared eight years ago, when he was six. Troubled kid from a lazy family. Went to St. Alfred's, too, just like Stanley. Only thing people really remembered about him is that he had a nice voice."

The organ music stopped playing and I glanced up at the organ loft. Mr. Trevor, looking well in a black robe, stood up to leave. Suddenly something clicked into place. Or rather a bunch of somethings that had seemed like nothing at the time.

I turned my back to him and said to Terrence in a low voice, "We gotta question the organist. Now. He's the music teacher at the pre-school, was here when Stanley disappeared and..." This is what I had realized when I saw Trevor in his robes. "Aunt Mavis says he comes from a terrible family, and Tasia shies away from him. I wonder if...." I wondered if Mr. Trevor was abused himself as a child. I wondered if he'd become an abuser.

Terrence started walking swiftly to the back, and broke into a run once we were out into the hall. "Not sure of your reasoning, man," he said in a whisper as he ran, "But he's the best suspect we got right now." We reached the door to the organ loft just as Trevor was exiting.

"Mister Trevor," said Terrence, pulling out his badge, "I am Detective Jackson from the 35th Precinct. We would like to talk to you about the death of Sammy Dillon and the disappearance of Stanley Wilson."

Trevor wasn't a young man but he reacted instantly, disappearing back through the door and slamming it behind him. It locked tight and didn't budge when I rattled the handle.

"Find Rev. Cuthbert," said Terrence, "She'll have a key. I'm gonna find another way up there."

I nodded and ran back into the nave of the church. Antoine — or rather Sammy — was gone, but the Reverend was just putting her chalice away. "Reverend," I called as I ran up to her, "We have reason to suspect that Mister Trevor is guilty of a serious crime, but he's disappeared up the stairs of the organ loft. Do you have the key to that door?"

She nodded and started walking toward a small door behind the altar. "I have an extra set of keys in here." She unlocked a desk drawer and handed me a small silver key. "Be careful. It sticks," she said as I ran back into the main body of the church and out into the hall.

She was right. I cursed at the lock as I jiggled the key this way and that. It finally clicked and I started tearing up the dark steep stairs. There was a door to the organ loft but the stairs kept on going up beyond that. I kept climbing until I reached a set of metal stairs and what was obviously a door to the roof. I didn't think he would be waiting for me but I listened carefully before opening it. I heard nothing, so turned the knob and pushed the heavy door out on to the roof.

Terrence had managed to find another way up, and I could see him and Trevor silhouetted in the last light of that December dusk.

"I'm going to die anyway," Trevor was saying.

"HIV is not a death sentence," Terrence responded in his talking-to-a-crazy-person voice. "These days people got good drugs. My uncle would still be alive if he could have gotten the cocktails they got today."

"Sammy's dead, and Stanley is a little bastard," were

Trevor's last words as he stepped off the edge of the roof.

"Crap," said Terrence. It was obviously the most useful word in his current vocabulary. He turned to me. "Is Elvis the Queen still around? We could use a coroner." A thin wail of a siren split the cold air. "And there's my backup coming. Lemme go down and see the results."

I nodded. "And I'll poke around here in case the little bastard happens to be here." I called Elvis, who was indeed not far away, and told him about Trevor jumping. Then I went down to the preschool to see the wall that Trevor had been working on when I dropped Tasia off last week. When I looked closely, I could see a small dent about the size of a preschooler's boot that had been spackled over by Trevor. Maybe Stanley was somewhere nearby.

Tasia saw me and left her work to come see what I was doing. Given how good her instincts were, I told her I was trying to figure out where Stanley was.

"Maybe he upstairs," said Tasia. "I heard somebody yelling, but the teachers didn't believe me."

We walked back behind the classroom and found a bunch of doors. Most of them were closets or small offices with nothing but dust bunnies. But after four or five tries we found a set of stairs going up. The room led to an abandoned corridor. I tried to flip on a light but nothing happened when I tried the switch next to the stairs.

"I hear a TV," said Tasia, pointing down the hall. I

grabbed her hand, probably as much for my comfort as hers, and we walked down the hall together. In a couple of steps, I, too, could hear the sounds of some violent cartoon program. At the end of the hall was a door barricaded by a large table. We called through the door but the TV was too loud to tell if somebody was answering. I pushed the table away and then opened the door.

I heard scrambling as I pulled the door towards me, and ducked a mug being thrown at me as soon as I got the door open a couple of inches.

"Stop throwing things at my dad!" yelled Tasia when she saw what was happening.

I gingerly opened the door the rest of the way and saw in the dim light Stanley in the middle of a pile of empty bottles of coke and cookie packets, holding a plate to throw at me despite his hands being duct taped together in front of him and his ankles taped together as well.

"You okay, Stanley?" I asked, ready to duck the plate as well.

He put dropped the plate and thought about this question. "I think so," he finally said. "I scared away Creepy Mr. Trevor, didn't I?"

I grinned. "You did indeed. Good job. Not a lot of kids could do that. He was a really bad man."

Stanley seemed pleased and smiled back.

"Stanley's a hero!" yelled Tasia.

Stanley's smile grew broader and somehow shyer at the same time. "Wha's up, Tasia?"

"You gonna hit me again if my dad takes off that tape?" she asked in response, still wary of him even now.

"Nope," he said.

Tasia looked at him hard.

"I promise, really promise," he said, very earnestly.

"Okay, dad," she responded. "You can let him out."

I kept my face as straight as possible during this exchange. She was as forthright as her mama about what she wanted.

"I'm gonna have to carry you downstairs to find some scissors, Stanley."

"Okay, Mr. Claw," he said.

Carrying even a small kid like Stanley with his hands and feet together is awkward, but with Tasia opening doors in front of me, we made it out of the gloom upstairs and down into the bright light downstairs. The light of the pre-school and all the colors on the walls was almost blinding. The other kids had gone home but somehow their presence still lingered. Miss Tonya and Miss Elma came running when we came through the door.

"Stanley stopped that creep!" announced Tasia

triumphantly.

"You did good, honey," said Miss Elma, "Real good. Your mama and granmama gonna be real glad to see you."

Stanley shrugged at this, but did sit still enough long enough to let me cut his legs and arms free. He started jumping up and down like a basketball player warming up. I figured he earned it, even though I winced every time his arms came near something. We all started making phone calls. I called Terrence, Miss Elma called Mrs. Wilson and Miss Tonya called Stanley's mom. Once the cries of perhaps muted joy from the other end of the phones had died down, Stanley asked the most pertinent question.

"So what happened to Creepy Mr. Trevor?" He asked.

"I'm afraid he's dead," I answered, sorry to not be able to mourn this man even a little.

"Good," said Stanley and Tasia simultaneously, and then laughing together.

"Jinx!" yelled Tasia and that shut up Stanley for a little while until Tasia released him from it.

Miss Tonya brought us all snacks. Tasia took a cookie, but Stanley went for an apple. "I seen enough cookies for a while," he said in explanation.

After a while, Miss Tonya's voice broke into the desultory chatter involved in waiting for others to arrive.

"Oh," she said. "Our Christmas pageant is Thursday

and Mr. Trevor was supposed to play Santa Claus."

"Don't worry," said Tasia. "Daddy was born to play Santa Claw."

A THEFT OF TEAPOTS

by

Cris de Borja

"Marin, thank you for coming over. You drove?" Mrs. Sugiyama held the door open for her neighbor. A toffee-colored pit bull terrier danced behind the lady of the house.

Marin Quinn stepped inside. "This cold still has me dragging my feet," she explained, not without embarrassment. Kiyomi Sugiyama, in spite of her eighty-some years, thought nothing of walking all over Eagle Crest. Marin was less than half her age and had not been up to the hillside hike between her home and her neighbor's.

As Marin slipped off her shoes, she held a hand out, and Sweetpea pushed her head against Marin's fingers. The dog fell to the floor, rolled on her back to show her spotted belly, and wriggled. Marin couldn't help laughing.

Her hostess took Marin's hooded jacket to hang it up.

"Are you warm enough in this?" The elderly woman fussed. "It's so thin."

"It's a high tech design. It's a lot warmer than it looks, honestly."

"Wool is heavy but you can count on it," the older woman advised. "Come in, sit down. I went by the bakery this morning so we can have kringle with our tea." She ushered Marin through the parlor's open door.

The room was clean but cluttered with objects that didn't belong. Mrs. Sugiyama's forgetfulness carried household items to strange shores. A bath brush, a kitchen colander, and one of Sweetpea's dishes—with kibble—as well as more ordinary things such as books and magazines lay where they had been set down for a moment and then forgotten.

Marin found a seat after moving a library book on flower arranging. "It's nice to sit on a different couch," she joked. "All I've been able to do since picking up this bug is sit in my living room and watch videos of cats on my laptop. For weeks! I even missed the Tea Festival, and the opening of the new art gallery. Since her shop carries my pottery, Anne from *Two for Tea* expected me to help run her booth at the festival. Emily had to take my place."

Mrs. Sugiyama tipped her head. "That's right. I saw your niece minding their table. That new boyfriend she has was distracting her."

"He's been around a lot lately. Kiyomi? You said that you needed my help with something?"

"A thief broke into my house last night."

"What?" Marin sat up straighter. "Are you all right? Where was Sweetpea? You reported it, didn't you?"

Mrs. Sugiyama hesitated. "You are so good at finding answers for some of the odd happenings here in Eagle Crest," she started, absentmindedly patting her short, grey hair while she plucked a lacquered hair stick out from between cushions.

"I thought you might be more help."

Marin cringed. When she moved to the mountain town of Eagle Crest to pursue her pottery full time, she hadn't intended to become an amateur sleuth on top of it. It wasn't her fault that she kept getting mixed up in the town's mysteries, but once she was, she just had to shape the clay of the problem until the answer took form.

"What happened?" Marin asked.

"I was walking Sweetpea after dinner. When we returned home, Sweetpea started barking and pulling at her leash. I thought she was after a skunk again. Then we came inside, and I saw that the kitchen door was wide open. Sweetpea was barking at a different kind of skunk. She must have scared the thief away."

"What was stolen?"

"Teapots!" Mrs. Sugiyama exclaimed.

"Were they valuable?"

"I don't imagine they were. Only sentimental value." She reached under the coffee table and brought up a cardboard shipping box. "I am glad that I forgot to put this one away." The box had the word nickels written in marker on one side. She lifted a porcelain teapot with pale green enamel out of its wrapping of tissue, setting aside the separately wrapped lid.

"What a lovely teapot," Marin said.

"It was in the History of Tea display at the Tea Festival." She placed it back into the box. "My dear old friend Lily was very active with the Tea Society." Mrs. Sugiyama was quiet for a moment, and then said, "I have a wonderful chrysanthemum herbal that will be good for your cold, Marin. I am sure this old teapot will be happy to be put to use."

"Kiyomi, do you think this is what the thief was after?" Marin asked, indicating the old teapot.

"It couldn't have been this particular one. I haven't had it long."

"But this is Kutani porcelain," said Marin. "Even newer pieces from the Kutani region are popular in the antique market, and this looks mid-century or older."

"Mid-century? Is that what the 1950's are called now?" The octogenarian smiled. "Well, you are right. Mother gave this teapot to my friend Lily's parents as a thank you, after the end of the war, for the help her family gave to mine. If not for them, we wouldn't have had even a teacup left to come home to, let alone our house."

Marin didn't have to ask what she was talking about. Kiyomi Sugiyama would have been a young girl when the U.S. entered World War II. Her family would have been one of many that were sent to internment camps. In a few cases, non-Japanese Americans held homes, businesses, and possessions in stewardship until their friends could reclaim them. Mrs. Sugiyama's matter-of-fact reference to that history somehow made Marin feel worse about the families that did lose everything. Feeling guilty about steering the conversation back to a safer topic, she asked, "Were your other teapots family heirlooms, too?"

"Oh, no. They were ordinary ceramic and wouldn't sell for a dollar at a yard sale. Even the lids were mismatched. I gave all the good ones to my daughters and daughter-in-law. When I make tea for myself I rarely brew a whole pot. But Connie Jimenez said she saw her stolen teapot on that internet auction place. She says it's bone china, but she also says 'wu long' instead of 'oolong'."

"She had a teapot stolen too?"

"Haven't you heard about the break-ins?" Mrs. Sugiyama asked. "Amy Bevins lost a whole set still in the box from *Two for Tea*. Gavin James had a window smashed, and his china cabinet broken into. Judy and Kay told me that they had all three of their teapots taken. That nice real estate lady had one of those cute little English teapots with the stacking cup, and that was stolen from her office right in the middle of the day."

"Kiyomi, have you been interviewing the victims?" Marin was dismayed. Sheriff Brower had issued several stern warnings to Marin about amateur crime investigation. Julie Brower would not tolerate an epidemic of part-time detectives.

"We're all in the Tea Society," Mrs. Sugiyama said.

She took the teapot, leaving the box behind, into the

kitchen. Sweetpea rose from her deceptive nap to follow. Mrs. Sugiyama came out a moment later with a sheet of paper. Sweetpea returned with her. "This is a picture from the internet of the teapot that Connie says is hers."

Marin took a look. "It's just the photo." Her hostess looked at her with confusion. "It doesn't have any information about the listing," Marin explained. "No header for the web address, none of the text that went with the image."

"Is that no good?"

"No, I'm afraid not. She must have selected 'print image' instead of printing the page."

"She couldn't figure out how to work the printer. Her child uses the printer all the time so she had him do it."

"It sounds like you don't think she's telling the truth."

"It wouldn't be Connie's first creative embellishment. She knows about the break-ins. If everyone is wearing birthday hats, she has to be the birthday girl."

Marin studied the image. "I can look up this copyright watermark." She dug into her skirt pocket and pulled out her phone and a few stray cherry cough drops. After returning the cough drops, she turned on her phone and poked at the screen.

Mrs. Sugiyama raised her eyebrows. "That's like a tiny computer, isn't it? With a video camera, too?"

Marin nodded as she pecked out a search. "I'm looking up the seller's name from the watermark. Here it is." She stopped to look at the elderly Mrs. Sugiyama. "How did you know these took video?"

"At the festival, your niece's beau was on his soapbox about how important the latest technology is. The usual nonsense that we all think when we are youngsters. He had a phone like yours. When he started taking photographs with it, Emily shooed him away."

"She hates getting her picture taken." Marin turned her attention back to her mobile phone's screen. "This seller looks legitimate. Top rated seller, lots of transactions, and orders ship from New Jersey." She looked up at her neighbor. "I don't think this is Connie's teapot either, but I'll save this information to look into further." Marin was about to slip her phone away when a message notification trilled.

"I'll bring out the tea things if you want to take that call," Mrs. Sugiyama offered.

"No, it's a text from Emily. She needs the car to drive her boyfriend Nathan back to the city."

"Why not invite her to tea? If she's not in a rush," she added.

"That would be nice. Thank you." Marin tapped the invitation message to her niece, received a fast reply, and passed the response along.

"I should start some hot water." Mrs. Sugiyama said.

"Emily won't be here for a few minutes yet."

"After the second one happened, I told Emily's young man—Nathan, was it?—that these burglaries were news. Wasn't he trying to get a job with the Register?"

"It fell through," answered Marin, restraining herself from gossiping.

She'd heard the story directly from Bill, the newspaper's editor, and it was one of the reasons that Marin didn't like the boy for Emily. Nathan had been on the newspaper of his university until he was kicked off for submitting an altered photo to support a story. He then falsified a letter of recommendation to Bill. Bill had the impression that the young man was too impatient to do real reporting. He called the boy a corner-cutter.

"Hmm. Anthea Clark and Holly Yoder both said that he 'invited himself' to tea at their houses to interview them, even though neither of their houses was robbed. I suppose none of us can turn down a request to bring out our teapots." Mrs. Sugiyama added, "If only Holly Yoder had more people over for tea to listen to her ideas, we would have an independent party mayor after this election."

"I like Holly, too, but she doesn't have the financial backing that either Hoffman or Kort has," said Marin. "What can you tell me about the other burglaries?"

"They started last week. The night after the Tea Festival, a thief broke into *Two for Tea*. Walter Hall—he lives above his bookstore, across the street from the shop—saw a strange car parked behind the diner and called the sheriff's office. The thief got away before the deputy roused himself. Anne's bookkeeping files were a mess, she said."

"Can Mr. Hall identify the car?"

Mrs. Sugiyama shook her head. "Walter's eyes aren't what they used to be."

"Hello..." Emily, poking her head in, called through the back door as she opened it. She beamed when she saw Mrs. Sugiyama and Marin in the kitchen. The rest of her, a plump figure in t-shirt and jeans, sidled through the kitchen door without opening it fully. Her cheeks were pink from activity and the cold day. "Thank you for having me over. I hope it's OK that I brought a plus-one. Nathan is still hiking up. The dangers of smoking," she laughed. When she caught Marin's look she quickly added, "He's quitting. He chews gum instead."

Sweetpea wiggled toward the newcomer, tail wagging, but stopped short with an abrupt bark. Emily looked concerned. "Oh no, sweetie," she crooned. "It's me. What's the matter?"

Mrs. Sugiyama shushed at the pit bull. "She's been out of sorts all morning." She grabbed the dog's collar and guided her toward the inner doorway. "Go on to your room, Sweetpea," she ordered. The pit bull obediently went to the front of the house. "I can't think of anything that she needs to do," she said euphemistically. She followed Sweetpea through the parlor and closed the door between the parlor and the front of the house.

Emily had a grass-green political button on the wide strap of her purse. She took two more of the "Grassroots for Holly" buttons out of her purse and handed them to her aunt and her neighbor. "You'll support Holly Yoder for mayor, won't you?"

"Do you think she has a real chance, Emily?" Marin asked. "Third party candidates are either ignored or they muddle the vote."

"That's no reason to vote for Celeste Kort. Or Todd Hoffman," Emily stated. "They were both at the gallery opening, sucking up to all the rich people. Neither of them bothered to come to the Tea Festival, even though we were right next door to the gallery. But their security guys went through the festival like the chase scene in a spy movie. They actually have bodyguards, can you believe that?"

"I have to agree with Emily, Marin," said Mrs. Sugiyama. "Neither of them is from our town. I can't imagine why either wants to be our mayor. They're city people. No offense to you two," she hurried to add.

"I was sorry to miss the gallery party," said Marin, redirecting the subject.

"I was sorry to miss it, too, since I was stuck working the booth for my sick auntie," Emily joked. "That turned out OK, though."

"Oh," said Marin. "Hey, kiddo, that reminds me. Could you get my car emptied? There is still stuff from the festival in the car."

"Of course, Aunt Marin. Nathan can help me drop it off at *Two for Tea* before we head down to Everett. I'll even fill up the tank," she added brightly. "My bag is full of buttons to give out," she confided in a conspiratorial voice.

Looking more closely at the slogan button, Marin asked, "Did you design these? They look great."

"I'm keeping busy," Emily replied. "The buttons are a donation to Holly Yoder's campaign, but my T-shirt is for work."

"What's twenty four?" asked Marin, looking at the oversized number on the bold red T-shirt.

"Two. Four. It's a two four tee. A *Two for Tea* shirt," she explained. Although she did not actually roll her eyes, she wore a look that implied that her aunt was a hopeless case.

Surprised, Marin asked, "When did you get a job with the tea shop?"

"Because I worked the festival table, Anne hired me for our marketing and other stuff. I'm designing new T-shirts to sell online," said the girl, pulling her top straight over her ample curves to show off the logo. "I'm doing a series of designs that will give *Two for Tea* a fresh look. There are lots of younger people getting into tea, and we need to appeal to that market." She teased her aunt, "Where did you think I'd been going all week?"

"I thought you were spending time with Nathan," Marin replied, thinking about how often she had seen the boyfriend around during her week of living room convalescence. Marin tried hard not to pressure her niece with expectations while Emily lived with her. Emily had already run away from college; landing in Eagle Crest with her aunt was a temporary measure. Marin didn't want to push her niece into running further.

Emily continued, "Anne is still really upset about the break-in last week."

Marin grabbed the opportunity. "Has she said anything more about it?"

"Not really. But since they got into her files, she's finally joining the twenty-first century and putting that information on her computer so she can keep a backup. I already had the sales data from the festival in a spreadsheet. Anne was pretty impressed with that."

While her guests were conversing, Mrs. Sugiyama had filled the electric kettle and washed out the teapot. "Should we wait for Nathan before I start tea?" she asked.

"Where is he," Emily wondered aloud. "I'm going to see if he got lost coming up the one straight path from the house. You don't have to wait. I'll be right back."

Mrs. Sugiyama searched the cluttered countertop with a look of concern. "I've misplaced the lid," she said, puzzled.

"This lid from one of my covered teacups will do for now, but I do hope I haven't lost the right one already."

"Is it still in the box?" Marin suggested. She went into the other room with her hostess to check.

The kitchen door opened. This time, Emily came in with a skinny young man with a backpack who lingered at the doorway. Emily instructed him to take off his shoes, as she was doing, and put them on a shelf by the door. He rewarded her with a look of incredulity.

"There are house slippers if you want," Emily cajoled in a small voice that could still be heard clearly in the parlor.

"We should get going."

"OK, but we have to drive my Aunt Marin back to her house, first. We have to put the stuff in the back seat into the trunk to make room."

"I'll do that," he quickly volunteered. "I can put my stuff in the car. Can you get me the keys?"

"Nathan, can you show Aunt Marin the pictures from the Tea Festival?"

"They were on the phone that I lost, Emily." Nathan fidgeted.

"The car is usually unlocked," Marin said, "but I'll go get my keys. They're still in my coat."

"I can get them for you, Marin," Mrs. Sugiyama offered. She puttered out into the hallway. In a moment, she was back with Marin's coat. Emily took the car keys to Nathan and returned.

The box on the low table caught Emily's curiosity. "That's my writing," she said, indicating the lettering in marker. "I packed up the displays after the Tea Festival. How did Dave's box end up here?" she wondered. "Did you hear about Dave Nickels by the way? When his house got robbed, the burglar hit him over the head. He had to go down to United General for an MRI or CAT scan. One of those tests to make sure you don't have brain damage."

"That's dreadful!" Mrs. Sugiyama exclaimed. "When did it happen?"

"He was robbed last week," said Emily. "Actually, he was the first house robbery after the break-in at the store."

"I can't imagine why he didn't say anything about it when he came by," said Mrs. Sugiyama. "Dave Nickels is Lily's grandson," she explained to Marin. "I just saw him yesterday afternoon. He is a nice young man, a little odd, but well-mannered. He only drinks coffee, isn't that strange? He doesn't care for tea."

Marin connected the surname to the writing on the box. It made more sense than a box full of five cent coins, although the fellow in town who kept pennies in mason jars came to mind. Marin belatedly realized that she needed to ask Mrs. Sugiyama for more details of how she came to acquire the Kutani teapot.

Mrs. Sugiyama took Marin's coat back to the coat rack, waving off Marin's intent to do so herself. When she came back, she left the connecting door open behind her for a moment before she remembered Sweetpea. She was about to close the door when the dog rocketed out.

Sweetpea tore through the parlor and straight for the kitchen like a bullet. Her barking and Nathan's yelling clashed in a cacophony of alarm.

The women, all following in a hurry, stampeded into the kitchen. Pressed into a corner and wearing a look of total panic, Nathan used a kitchen chair for a shield. Sweetpea barked and growled, looking scarier than Marin had ever seen her.

Instead of quieting down when Mrs. Sugiyama scolded her, she moved in front of the old woman protectively and continued to threaten Nathan.

Nathan's backpack sat unzipped on the floor, flap open like a tongue to reveal unusual ceramic teeth, including a newly added porcelain one: an assortment of teapots. The teapots fought for space with Nathan's packed clothes. Rumpled shirts padded the ceramic surfaces from knocking against each other.

"Hey!" exclaimed Marin indignantly. "One of those is mine!" She removed Mrs. Sugiyama's green teapot frst, placing it gently back on the counter. She continued unpacking the backpack. The other teapots lined up next to the porcelain one like chorus girls.

"You're the thief!" Mrs. Sugiyama said. "Sweetpea can smell your cologne! She doesn't like smells like that." She turned to Emily. "The smell was on you, too, when you came in the door."

Marin addressed the young man. "It doesn't look good, Nathan."

"Please call off the dog already!" Nathan begged. "I can explain everything!"

Mrs. Sugiyama tried to get Sweetpea calmed, but the pit bull kept barking until Marin moved around the kitchen table to Nathan's side and got him to put down the chair. He stood warily behind it, eyeing the dog. Sweetpea eyed him back.

"What's to explain?" huffed Mrs. Sugiyama. "Those are the teapots that were stolen from me last night. And Marin? You said that the other one is yours?"

"That's the one I brought you from the Tea Festival," Emily noted sadly. "Nathan, I know you need money, but that's not worth anything resale. It's just commemorative."

The old woman pointed to her landline telephone on the wall. "Pick up that phone and turn yourself in," she fumed. "The sheriff's number is right there next to it, where I keep my emergency numbers."

Nathan opened his mouth to speak. He stopped short

when Sweetpea growled loudly. Any time that Mrs. Sugiyama moved, Sweetpea moved to keep herself between her owner and Nathan.

Beaten, Nathan picked up the heavy plastic receiver of the old telephone. He stared at the rotary dial, looking miserable. "How do you use this artifact?" he complained. He backed away from Sweetpea when Mrs. Sugiyama took the receiver.

Mrs. Sugiyama dialed the rotary phone for him, shaking her head all the while. Once she confirmed that the sheriff's office was on the line, she handed the receiver back to Nathan.

Over the phone, Nathan admitted to his crimes without elaboration. He stated where he was and then hung up. He hadn't needed to give the address; the sheriff knew all of Marin Quinn's neighbors.

He looked around from face to face. "It wasn't about money," he said.

"I think you had better tell your story from the beginning," Marin suggested to Nathan.

He sat down with the table between him and Sweetpea. "There was that art gallery event going on at the same time as the Tea Festival. I was bored, and I went over to see if there was a more interesting news story there. I followed Todd Hoffman, one of your candidates for mayor, for a while. He was talking to one of the bigwigs pushing that new pipeline.

Of course, that's no surprise. It's politics as usual. Here's the thing, though. Later, I saw that same person having a secret meeting with Celeste Kort. That's when I started taking video, with my phone."

Marin asked, "I take it this was not out in public. Celeste Kort has her business office in that same building, doesn't she?"

Nathan continued. "They left separately, but I followed them to the corridor. Hoffman joined them, and they all talked together. The corporate suit left them at the elevator, grinning like he'd won the Lotto. Then it got even better. Kort and Hoffman didn't even wait until the elevator doors closed before they were all over each other."

Marin was taken aback. "What?"

"They're having an affair. They must be helping each other, or the election is fixed or something. Hoffman and Kort aren't who they say they are. My journalistic instinct was right! No one can say I photoshopped this story. I found news that would make my career! Would, if I could find the SD card," he corrected. "I tried to email the file to myself but there wasn't any signal." He grimaced. "I had barely enough time to hide the micro SD and run."

"You hid the memory card from your smart phone in a teapot," Marin concluded. "That's why you've been stealing teapots."

"It's on the bottom of a lid," Nathan said, "I stuck it

under the paper of one that was already packed up." Nathan slunk down in his chair. "The boxes were labeled. I thought I would remember which one I stuck it into. Except it wasn't there, so I kept looking. It wasn't on any of them." He studied the line of teapots on the counter.

"The lid!" Marin snapped her fingers. "Kiyomi, we were looking for that." She ran out to the parlor and came back with the cardboard box that the Kutani teapot had been in. She fished around and found the bundle of paper wrapping.

Marin unwrapped the teapot lid. As most of the paper came off, Mrs. Sugiyama made a noise of dismay. Marin made a face. A wad of chewing gum plugged the lid's inner contour.

"Kiyomi, you don't mind if I help myself to some ice, do you?" she asked. "And a zippy bag? I can get this gum off, I think."

Mrs. Sugiyama handed over a freezer bag of frozen roadside blackberries. "Will these do?" she asked. "It's these or freezer jam."

"I'll take the bag," Marin laughed.

Mrs. Sugiyama turned to Nathan. "How did you decide to start breaking into houses?" she asked. "I wouldn't think a visitor would know which homes belonged to members of our Tea Society."

The man shrugged.

Marin pulled out a chair and sat down near Nathan.

"Emily had a customer list on her laptop," she said, looking at her niece for confirmation. She applied the icy bag to the clump of gum inside the lid.

The girl blinked rapidly. "The spreadsheet I made for Anne." She looked at Nathan. "You didn't."

"Here we go," Marin interrupted. She picked the hardened gum off in a clump, handed the lid to Mrs. Sugiyama, and pried a tiny black chip away from the gum. It came away cleanly.

"That tiny thing is what you wanted so badly?" Mrs. Sugiyama asked. "If Constanza Jimenez had that on her Made in China teapot, it would have gone down the drain of her dishwasher!"

Marin took out her phone. "I'm not sure if I should be doing this," she said as she carefully removed the back of the case. Trying not to jostle the battery or the SIM card that held her phone's identity, she removed the micro SD card that stored photos and music.

She set her original card carefully onto the tabletop. She picked up the other tiny rectangle of memory, checked it for gum residue, and popped it into her phone. The backing snapped onto her phone with a click. Turning her mobile phone back on, she added, "Now let's see what's on here."

Marin poked at her phone's touchscreen. "Lots of photos..." She flicked through them. They were all images from a crowded event, including stills of the mayoral candidates. "This one is video." A tap started the video file.

Mrs. Sugiyama leaned toward the tiny screen and watched. "Shameless," she commented when the playback finished.

Marin tapped her fngers against her lips as she thought. "Todd Hoffman is known for his rhetoric on the sanctity of marriage, and Celeste Kort has been slinging mud at Hoffman about environmental issues since the beginning of their campaigns. Publicly, they hate each other. The voters might forgive the extramarital affair even if the spouses don't, but with everything else, it smells rotten."

Nathan pitched to Marin's sympathy. "Their security guys chased me to the tea thing where Emily was closing up. After I hid the card, I kept running. They took my phone and smashed it, and they would have smashed me up, too, if I hadn't gotten away again. That vid is important! People need to see the truth. I need that chip," Nathan pleaded. "When I break that story, I guarantee that a major news network —"

"Nathan, it's too late for that," Marin said. "You've committed burglary and assault. Serious crimes."

As if summoned, Sheriff Brower knocked on the front door. In short time, she put Nathan into the back of her vehicle and drove away. Emily rode with them in a sudden rush of pity for her criminal boyfriend. When they were gone, Sweetpea curled up by the heat register, appearing in every way to nap while Mrs. Sugiyama was nearby.

Marin sighed from her place by the front room window as she watched them go. Julie Brower had not said a word to Marin, but the sheriff's look, upon seeing Marin Quinn involved, had spoken volumes.

"After the way this morning has gone, Kiyomi, I think we could both use that cup of tea now."

Mrs. Sugiyama nodded. "I heartily agree. And greenie biscuits for my good girl," she promised Sweetpea.

While the tea brewed, Marin watched the video again. "It's a good, clear image, right up until the security goons noticed," she said to Mrs. Sugiyama as they drank soothing tea. She shook her head with regret for Nathan. Her index finger tapping against her lips, she wondered, "What should we do?"

"I don't know, Marin. Would Bill be able to do anything with that?"

"The Register is print-only, and I somehow think there would be reasons that Bill couldn't use this video. I could email it as an attachment, I guess, to everyone that I know in town. Someone would be able to use it." She looked at the small screen of her phone. "In spite of everything, I want Nathan Dugger to get credit for this," she realized.

Kiyomi tilted her head. "How?"

"Well..." said Marin, stalling while she was distracted with her phone. The keyboard was very small, but luckily her login and password for the website that she wanted were short and simple. After all, it was a website for hosting funny cat videos and similar clips, not her online banking website. When the video from the micro SD card started downloading to the website, she returned her attention to Kiyomi. "Well, that should do it," she said. "I'm putting the video up now. The hosting website provides a link that I can share online. The important bit is the description I'm going to write to go with the video, before I share it with the Eagle Crest neighborhood blog. Nathan Dugger will get the credit."

She said, "With Celeste Kort and Todd Hoffman's shenanigans exposed, I anticipate that they're going to lose the support of their respective political parties. Maybe we will get an independent party mayor after all."

"Holly Yoder would make a good mayor. Let's drink to that, why not?"

"It's a little soon to celebrate," Marin laughed.

"Ah no, Marin," said the gray-haired woman. "Every day is a reason to celebrate, all on its own." She refilled their cups from her heirloom Japanese teapot.

"So let me see if I figured it all out," Marin announced. "Nathan hid his video recording in the lid of this teapot, after the Tea Festival. He broke into *Two for Tea* that night, expecting to get it back. But it had already gone back to its owner, Dave Nickels," she said. She savored a sip of chrysanthemum tea. "Nathan remembered the name on the box. When he couldn't find it, he rifled through Anne's files, looking for more information, but Anne has years' worth of filing and probably her own magical system for finding things in it. Then Nathan discovered that Emily had a spreadsheet with just the information that he needed."

She waded back in. "Nathan was still chasing the right box when he burgled Dave Nickels's house. He didn't find the teapot there. That's when he started second guessing himself about what he remembered. He also tried another tactic: 'interviewing' the others on the list at tea time, hoping to find it that way. He had plenty of time, with Emily as an excuse for him to be in town for the week, even though Emily was busy working. Plus, Emily was willing to be his driver, so he could leave his car at home, the strange car that Walter Hall identified as being parked nearby when *Two for Tea* was burgled. I'll bet that he used Emily's bicycle to get around Eagle Crest at night. He could only carry a few teapots in his backpack at a time."

"It was an odd thing to do, taking all those teapots. I wonder what he did with them."

"What I'm not sure about is how he tracked it back to you. I think he did, however. I think that stealing my teapot today was an act of absolute desperation, fueled by the opportunity of my being out of the house. We—Sweetpea, that is—caught him in the act today when he saw that there was another teapot here that he hadn't seen last night."

"Honestly, Marin, when I saw this teapot in the History of Tea display, I didn't recognize it after all these years. I was surprised when Lily's grandson arrived at my door yesterday. I knew who he was, but he hasn't been social. He only ever comes to our town to work on fixing up Lily's old house, so that he can sell it."

"But he brought you the teapot."

"He said that he wanted me to have it back." Mrs. Sugiyama smoothed her hair.

"Why?" Marin asked.

"He wanted to do the right thing. When he found the teapot in the house, he misunderstood. He thought it was a family shame, that his great-grandparents had kept some of the property that they promised to hold for us. I explained everything. He still wanted me to keep it, so that it would be in use."

"That's how you ended up with the hidden SD card. I think Nathan either followed Dave Nickels or saw him going to or coming from your house."

"And so, here we are," Mrs. Sugiyama finalized.

"Here we are," Marin agreed. She stood up, thinking that it was time for her to end the visit.

"Let me walk you to your car, Marin," said Mrs. Sugiyama. "It's about time for Sweetpea and me to get some fresh air and exercise. I hear that we can expect snow in the next few days." She headed to the front door with her guest.

They put on shoes and coats. Sweetpea held still for her

leash to be clipped on, but was eager to go as soon as they opened the door.

Marin saw the festival banner and other items that were still in the back seat of her car. "I'm just going to put those in the trunk now," she commented to her neighbor. She turned the key. "I'll get them to Anne when I see her next." She lifted the lid of the trunk open.

"What is it, Marin?" Mrs. Sugiyama voiced concern at Marin's face.

"I found the stolen teapots," laughed Marin. "Can you believe the nerve? He was hiding them in my car!"

STORM OF MYSTERY

by

Leonhard August

It was early morning when Dr. Dana Gibbs cleared immigration in the monorail station at the foot of the mountain. *Waw Gi:wulk*, Pinched Rock Mountain, was the first stop for all visitors. The Tohono O'odham Tribe had strict policies governing who was allowed onto the Nation's lands, and for non-O'odham, they dictated the terms of their visit.

Her job offer as Associate Research Director at the Center acted as her passport. In fact, folks seemed to treat her like an honored guest after they saw Dr. Miguel's signature on the old fashioned, honest-to-god-paper letter. One of the workers escorted her to the Center's dedicated elevator and used a passkey to unlock the button that sent the car directly to the top floor.

The elevator discharged her into an expanse of open office populated by comfortable chairs and a large table, and surrounded by floor-to-ceiling windows. Outside, the Sonoran desert spread out all around them in a carpet of tans, russets, and pale, faded greens—not the usual colors of winter in Chicago where she'd just come from, but beautiful nonetheless. She was surprised to find no reception desk waiting for her. She was even more surprised when the first person she'd encountered turned out to be the director of the Tohono O'odham Center for Advanced Computational Research himself.

"Excuse me," Dana said to the only person she could see in the vast space, an O'odham man with a round, barely-creased face and a jet braid untouched by gray. "Where can I find Dr. Miguel? I'm here for orientation."

The man turned from his display and smiled. "Then take two giant steps forward and stick out your hand. We don't stand on formality much here. You must be Dana. We're excited to have you aboard. NanoNeurology, right?"

"NanoNeurology. Uh, right." She said, while thinking, *that's why you hired me, Boss!*

He narrowed his eyes in a not unfriendly way and mumbled something under his breath. Had she known the O'odham language, she'd have realized he'd said, "And you're the one...so young."

"We've got great plans for you, Dana. Neuron models of data storage and manipulation. 'Our Next New Wave'. Sound interesting?" Seeing her startled look he went on. "Don't worry that you haven't heard about our activity in this area; it's not in the literature. We try to keep a lid on it, but it's the primary reason why we were so eager to have you join us here at the Center.

"We know that your University research on the Bio-Cyber project went beyond the noteworthy advances you described in your dissertation. It is our understanding that you conducted some, shall we say 'unauthorized' excursions into self-aware neural net processors."

Busted! Dana thought, wondering if they would try to set tighter limits for her on the new job.

"Don't blush, you won't face any restrictions here. We value tangential research as long as you keep your eyes on the prize, as they say." Dr. Miguel's eyes seemed to hold a conspiratorial smile.

"Your thesis advisor was shortsighted to make you stop your line of inquiry, but it's lucky for us she did. You were succeeding beyond, I might add, what we've been able to accomplish. Even more impressive, given that we are leading the field at this point. Now we get to turn you loose on a problem that was holding us back."

This just keeps getting better, Dana thought. *Turn me loose!*

His mien turned serious as he continued, "You know, of course, that it's an intense international race for the first position in this field. We haven't seen one this intense since the space race of the last century. To the victor in this race will go great spoils. We intend to be the victor, and to share our spoils with no one. Do you know much about us here the Center?"

"Data Haven, Secure Operations, and, of course, the associated research." Dana replied.

"Well, that's a good start." Dr. Miguel smiled again. "In the late twentieth century, Indian Gaming gave us the ability to not merely subsist as our ancestors had for thousands of years, but to again become self-sufficient. We invested in human capital first: food, education, and health care. Afterward, we invested in the future."

As Dr. Miguel went on to describe the origins of the Tribe's data storage and systems empire, Dana felt lucky she hadn't asked about the origins of the world; she had read that the O'odham Creation Story traditionally required four days to recount.

"Since the 18th century, tribes have operated as sovereign 'foreign' governments within the U.S. That's made us a legal pain in the...neck to some unfriendly administrations. I think some of them thought sovereignty would give them the excuse to cut off the tribes' access to Federal funding.

"Starting 20 or 30 years ago—early in the 21st century —we did everything we could to encourage this perception— in ways that were to our advantage, of course. As long as we weren't asking for anything, they were happy to leave us to our own devices. And this enabled us to build our 'off-shore' data depository." He chuckled, and then continued in falsetto. "Oh please, Br'er Bear! Don't throw me in de Briar Patch!"

Returning to his professorial tone, he continued, "By the time the Federal government finally pulled the plug on Indian gaming, we'd parlayed the profits into enough legislative influence to have the tribe's sovereignty affirmed, reaffirmed, and redefined in formal legislation. Even in the courts, from time to time." He continued with a twinkle in his eye, "There's a not-so-old O'odham saying that goes 'A good *Mediǵán* politician is one who stays bought after you've paid for him.' No offense intended," he added quickly, "*Mediǵán* is our generic name for Anglo white people.

"Now we're the Switzerland of data storage and a fortress for secure operations. We specialize in anonymity, speed, and security. Absolute performance for our client— absolute. We can make it better, faster, stronger, as the saying

97

goes. And we will do anything to protect our clients and our business."

"And the Center's role in the Tribe's strategic plan is to be the feet on the ground?" Dana asked.

"The Center develops new ways to harvest, store, and manipulate data. You might say our work is the grindstone that keeps the Tribe's cutting edge cutting." The smile widened to a grin.

Dana couldn't help but grin back. The O'odham had joined the white–*Medigán*–game, beat him at it, and were laughing all the way to the bank. She only hoped that she, as an outsider, wouldn't prove a disappointment.

"Forgive me, Dana." Dr. Miguel said suddenly. "You caught me on my way out the door. Our Chinese friends require my presence in Shanghai. But I do have something lined up for you to do on your own for the next couple of days."

Nothing like learning to swim by jumping off the deep end, Dana thought, but she said, "Wonderful. How do you want me to start? Will I be reading project reports? Meeting the team? Setting up facilities?"

"Regrettably, no. You'll have to delay your own work to help us with a priority project. We've got an immediate data security problem that we'd like you to tackle." He went on to describe that there had been low-level intrusion hacks that were both persistent and recurring. The Center's Security Staff had identified them, and the Associate Director for Security thought they were important to trace and neutralize.

"Unfortunately, the AD was on a cultural retreat in the desert when he was attacked by a rattlesnake. At the time, it didn't seem like it should be a fatal wound, but he proved to be particularly susceptible to the toxin and he passed on to the next world.

"We'd like you to start with the security issues he found, and shut down any threats. I saw from your official resume that you've been quite successful at that kind of work at your University." He said with the smile back in his eyes.

"I put together a summary of the security investigation for you. When you access your desktop, you'll see the summary file and a backup copy of the data files. It's not much, as I said, but it has a bad smell to it. I'd like you to read it before you go."

"Go?" asked Dana, "Go where?"

"You're going to have a cultural orientation starting later today. My assistant Madeleine has your paperwork down the hall."

Dana thought, *I came here for hardcore computing research, and start out by taking a field trip to the Reservation.* But she said, "Sounds...interesting," and hoped her disappointment didn't come through in her voice.

The director chuckled at her tone then fell serious. "With your credentials and shiny new doctorate, you've probably been beating off recruiters with a stick. Even so, you'd be no more than just another pair of hands to us if you didn't form your own understanding of this place and our people. This is our most sincere way of welcoming you, even if

99

it might not sound very productive right now. Take an hour or so to access your Desktop on the Center's system. I want you to look at those Security files." Dr. Miguel returned to packing his briefcase. Sensing dismissal, Dana muttered a polite goodbye and turned to go.

A young man brushed past her in the doorway. She continued out, ready to try and find Madeleine in the top-floor maze. She was vaguely aware that Dr. Miguel had greeted the man in the O'odham language, but their quiet discussion quickly faded and she heard no more.

❉   ❉   ❉

"*SKUG SIA:LIG*," Dr. Miguel said as the younger man approached. "Good morning, Oldest-Son-Of-My-Sister. That girl was the one we talked about. You will stay near her while she does her orientation. We don't want her to wind up as buzzard food. She has much yet to do for our People. The rattlesnake attack was a message—not just to the poor victim, but to us. We need to find the origin of the message and eliminate the threat."

"That brings me to the results of our investigation, Elder-Brother-To-My-Mother." The young man had known his uncle all his life, but politeness kept them from addressing one another by name. "As we suspected from the start, our man was not the victim of an ordinary creature. He was not allergic to snake venom, and the toxin itself was not potent enough to have killed him. The coroner found that something else was introduced with the snake bite, with deadly intent."

"But what of the EMT report? And the autopsy results?" Dr. Miguel interrupted.

"Accurate as far as they went, Uncle," the young man replied. "The anaphylactic shock was real. But it was a manufactured effect. It was caused by a very specific agent added to the natural venom."

"What?"

"The bite was faked. A synthetic venom was injected in such a way as to look like a real bite. We traced the source of the toxic agent—a small pharmaceutical lab outside of Kyoto. The company is controlled by one of the Zaibatsu."

"Which one?" Dr. Miguel asked. There were a dozen or so Japanese corporations of longstanding that had earned that title. "Was it that company that's trying to block our technology initiative with the Chinese?"

"Yes, Uncle."

Dr. Miguel shook his head. "I had hoped that our work would be simplified by the results of your investigation, not further complicated by them." Dr. Miguel said. "Why can't we just be attacked by Luddites, or the Neocons? It's simpler to deal with true believers than with money hungry BaBan." He used the O'odham word for coyotes. "EEYAH! It's getting harder with every new step we take." When he looked up again, his face was tired. "I say again. This thing must be done, now more than ever. Do what you must. The woman is the key. They won't wait long. I feel sure that tonight will be the night."

The young man usually reveled in the old-style speech

that speaking in O'odham forced upon the speaker, and the discipline it took to keep it up. Talking circles around everything, dancing around with indefinite references — it was poetic. And it forced the listener to really be present for the conversation. *Sometimes it just gives me a headache, though,* he thought. *Sometimes the Medigán style of "get to the point" works better. I need a cold drink.*

❀ ❀ ❀

DANA MET UP with Madeleine in a concealed hallway next to the Director's office. "Let me show you your spot, and get you accessed into the System." Madeleine said.

The shorter-than-usual, stouter-than-usual woman was probably in her forties, Dana thought, but could have passed for 30 or 50 in other circumstances. Her misty gray hair seemed to give her license to bustle, and bustle she did, swinging her arms like a hockey player. Never having spent time on skates, Madeleine had been proficient at O'odham field hockey, *Toka,* and as a girl had taken out her share of opposing fielders with those elbows.

Madeleine moved smoothly, though quickly, past offices, conference rooms and still more open areas and led Dana to a closed staircase marked Staff Only.

"Don't worry, honey," Madeleine chuckled as she said, "That's us. Quicker than going back to the elevators." And she led Dana one floor down.

Dana's "spot" was a large, private office in the Northeast corner, but still with a commanding view of the landscape below. The comfortable seating area had no visible desk, only a large captain's chair, five chairs for visitors, and the usual electronics well concealed as old-style office furniture.

Madeleine said, "The sensors can tell when you're in the room, and that it's you. No need to log in; it's biometric." She laughed at Dana's confused expression. "They scanned you downstairs, and in the elevator, and we got you coded in while you were talking with The Man. Sit down in your easy chair and you can start customizing your Desktop and displays. They're the usual virtual format, MAC-Win version two jillion or whatever. Just don't get too into it, I'll be back to get you in about an hour for your trip."

Settling in, Dana performed the usual electronic ablutions and rituals: email and calendar sync, ticklers loaded, personal site: check, check, check. Then she saw the "eyes-only" Security files the Director had left for her.

The summary showed that the former security chief (RIP) had sniffed out attempted intrusions to the Center's systems. The attacks were directed at remote access portals dedicated to support Center staff on offsite assignments. Not an uncommon strategy for typical hack attacks, but there were several aspects of the attempts that were not so typical.

As she dug into the traceback data on the attempts, they looked informed, not random. For one thing, the hackers took pains to originate the system access requests from locations geographically near to where Center staff were currently working. They were designed to resemble legitimate requests from staff working at home or offsite. That meant the intruders knew where and when Center staff were working offsite, even when that information was not public knowledge.

Second, the intrusions were almost perfect. They all had a single flaw in the code, though, that allowed the intrusion to be intercepted. It seemed to be planted deliberately to alert the snooper code in the Center's defense system.

Dana sat back, thinking. I've seen this before, in the attacks on the University systems—the attacks on my research.

Hacks had been reported on the University's support systems for the Bio-Cyber research team. Dana's personal research sectors and data, particularly her neural net research, had attracted much of the intruder activity. For that reason, she had been called in to assist in defense and countermeasures.

She remembered that each of the hacks had contained a telltale calling card that identified it as part of the campaign, an ID included almost as a point of pride. The same catch-me-if-you-can code and bravado was evident in the attacks on the Center. And again, they seemed to focus on the Bio-Cyber research support systems, the same activity that was targeted in Dana's work at the University.

The University had never identified the source or purpose of the attacks because her defense assignment had been cut short. The University President had announced that Bio-Cyber research would be conducted with a Japanese partner university, sponsored by a benevolent company—one of the Zaibatsu. "A Model of International Public/Private Co-operation for the benefit of mankind," he had called it. And then he had taken the Security investigation out of her hands and turned it over to their new partners.

The late lamented Security Chief of the Center had come close to identifying the attacks with the same Zaibatsu that co-opted the University research when he went on to Glory, Dana thought. But he couldn't connect the dots to our experience at the University. I can.

She sent a quick memo to the Director outlining a comparison of the hack attack on the Center with the one on the University. The notion that Bio-Tech related research was the target seemed obvious, now, and the high stakes associated with success to which Dr. Miguel had alluded made it more obvious.

She highlighted the fact that the epiphany represented by the Spirit of International Cooperation came to the University contemporaneously with the attack on its research computing systems. She didn't feel comfortable asking if the Center had been approached to share its research or to undertake a joint venture with the foreign firm, so instead she speculated that there might be a similar motive in play with the attacks on the Center.

Dana didn't know if her note would reach Dr. Miguel before he left for China, or before she herself left for her winter "summer camp" experience. She knew this little security problem would keep her mind occupied reexamining possibilities until she was able to get back on the system and do additional tracing and analysis of the intruder activity.

❈   ❈   ❈

"GRAB YOUR OVERNIGHT BAG, sister." Madeleine said when she came back to collect Dana an hour later. "As soon as I can get you a rig, you're on your way to the Zone—the CR."

"CR?" Dana asked, inexplicably feeling inadequate for having failed to bring an overnight bag to what was supposed to have been a job orientation.

"Cultural Reserve Zone. You'll have food and shelter, but no phone, no cable, no data, no 'net—nothing that didn't exist in the 19th century. AAaay—don't be afraid." The woman had laughed in response to her expression. "If you don't have a bag, the CR staff will fit you out from their office."

When she'd arrived at the Center, Dana had known that the traditional lands of the Tohono O'odham Nation comprised an area the size of a small U.S. state, that it was located above the Mexican Border, near Tucson, and that it had damn few non-O'odham residents. She knew their name meant desert people. But aside from this, and a handful of O'odham words, she hadn't known much else. She had the feeling she was going to find out a lot more, and soon.

Madeleine took her down to the CR office, a small building that looked desperately in need of paint and fixing-up, if not demolition and replacement. The staffer that met them looked like she could have been her guide's cousin, but she was introduced as "Miss Matilda, here, is my mother's very youngest sister, and that makes her my auntie. Hello auntie, What do you say — *Sa:p gaij?*"

"I don't have AN-Y-thin' to say, GUR-ull, at leas' 'til you introduce me to your FRIEN'." Matilda replied in the musical rhythm of the Reservation English they also called Medigán.

Matilda shared her niece's sturdy build, but she had the look of strength, the look of someone who spent a lot of time outdoors. Her functional, well-worn clothing had the same look, but a crisp, pressed appearance, too.

"'Tilly, this is Dana. Dana, 'Tilly. Happy now?" Madeline sighed. "She's a VIP from the Top Floors. We've gotta get her moving before the sun's too far up. Have you got her papers? Is she set up for a ride? Oh, and she's gonna need some clothes an' stuff, too."

"Yes, Your Majesty," Tilly drawled slowly, but without stopping. "Her place is ready, and I'm saddled up to take her out myself. Saddle bag's behind you with a hat, sunscreen, and hygiene kit. We'll get you into a long-sleeved T-shirt and jeans, and," looking at Dana's feet, "good shoes, and some unmentionables when you give us the sizes. And by the way, they're all yours to keep afterward, sweetie.

"Let's get movin'. You goin' out to 'The Palace', too Madeleine?"

"'Fraid not Auntie, duty calls from above."

Dana expected to see horses and pack mules, after Tilly had said she was "saddled up", but Tilly led her to a gravel parking lot. A line of ATV 4-wheelers sat in the sun, charging. The high efficiency solar panels powered their motors and replenished the batteries. They shaded the passengers, too, from the now-fiery rays of the sun.

"I thought technology was forbidden in the CR, the Zone." Dana said, catching up to Tilly.

Her new friend smiled briefly, then said, "There's technology, and then there's technology. We call these 'Sun Ponies' and the Council permits them all over the Res, even the Zone. The reasoning is that the Sun Pony isn't so different from a flesh and blood pony. The sun makes food for both of 'em and they can't carry much more than a couple of people and a pack. 'Sides, a Sun Pony don't try to bite you in the ass, and they're easier to clean up after.

❊   ❊   ❊

"MOUNT UP. We're in the one on the end. And PUT your HAT on, GUR-ull. You don't wanna fry your brains." Tilly said as she tossed the bag into the back of the Pony.

Food, furnishings and everything else were at the house. The Palace, the *gur-ulls* had called it. Good thing Dana hadn't brought a lot. There wasn't room for much. The sparse house had been built in the style of shelters used in traditional desert gathering camps. Ocotillo branches had been thrust into the soil around the perimeter of a shallow, circular pit to form the walls and ceiling. They were supported by a squarish frame of larger mesquite logs and branches. The square, the circle, and the dome occupied no more than a dozen square meters, and stood little higher than her head. The outside of the house had been covered much of the way down with loose earth, which had hardened into a weather barrier. The lower walls were covered with brush thickly enough that they kept out sun and rain, but loosely enough that they freely admitted moving air.

A sizable arroyo ran past the house into an open flat field. The field lacked trees of any size, marking it as a *vo'o*, a seasonal pond that held rainwater. After looking around the inside of the house, she'd stowed her gear on the narrow shelf that hung suspended by bear grass strips from the ocotillo stalks near the middle of the room. The shelf had yielded a brief, handwritten 'paper' about the house, its use, and its contents. It also pointed her to the food stores and kitchen utensils buried in the floor.

Winter meant that food and cooking depended on the preserved bounty of the intense summer growing season. Covered clay vessels were buried in the floor of the house. They contained dried beans, and dried corn, and a small amount of fat or shortening. Grinding stones, three battered pots, a fi-R-kit, another 'paper' with recipes, and three votive candles completed the outfit. She resolved to follow the pamphlet's instructions on preparing the food, thankful that she wasn't going to starve in a day regardless of her success — or lack of it — in the traditional ways of cooking.

A freshly filled *olla* of water rested in a cradle formed by three fingers of a branched mesquite log that was half buried in the floor. No O'odham dwelling would be without cool water for the dwellers and to offer visitors.

The rest of Dana's day was occupied with the tasks of subsistence. She cleaned the dried food of chaff, stones, and bugs. She ground some of the corn, slowly, by hand, and soaked some with the beans, to be boiled. She collected firewood and arranged it in the fire ring in front of the house. Just before the purple evening began, as the day faded, she dragged her sleeping mat outside, and dined as thousands before her had. But none better, she thought.

After supper, Dana wanted to relax and let her full belly put her to sleep, but her thoughts kept returning to the puzzle of the system attacks. The system incursions had been directed at specific research at both the University and at the Center: bio-cyber systems. Within that broader research area, they had been focused on her research area. No, they had zeroed in on her research.

Brilliant as my thesis was, she thought, *it's been fully published. No spying necessary. Hardly worth the time and effort the Zaibatsu seem to be devoting to it. My results were not revolutionary. Easily licensed and implemented from their university partner. What aspect of my work could possibly be worth stealing? Could it be my off-the-books development of a working neural net processor?* She wondered.

She made a mental note to have a full and frank discussion on the research area under attack at the Center with

Dr. Miguel. Was the Center working on neural processors? Self-aware processors?

Dana lay on the mat outside the house and tried again to sleep, thinking that the chill of night air would wake her later and tell her when it was time to go inside. Winter in the desert could send the temperature below freezing. Now, the air was still, but rather than turning cold, the night air was heavy, and her skin was humid, almost moist. On a winter evening, twilight is short, and it lacks the baked quality of the original solar oven. True night follows quickly after sunset and Dana was surprised by the appearance of the stars—so many stars. The half-moon was bright, but low in the sky. The slowly moving air touched her skin as she sat watching the sky, the desert, and the horizon.

Her eye was drawn to the flickering of dim lightning inside clouds, far away, almost out of sight. In Mexico, she thought. She thought of the Spanish, *la tormenta*. What was the O'odham word for storm, she wondered to herself, or were there many, like Inuit words for "snow"? Picking up her mat, she went inside to see if she could sleep better there.

If the clouds had been closer, she would have seen the texture of their black and white, boiling skin, lit from behind by the inner luminescence of cloud-to-cloud lightning. She couldn't tell when she'd finally fallen asleep, but when she awoke, the same flickering was the first sensation to register on her consciousness. Then the uncomfortable feeling of damp skin. At last, the deep, faint rumbling became connected in her thoughts to the flashes of light.

111

When she opened her eyes, the flashes lit the inside of the summer house dimly, briefly: without duration, without meaning. She closed her eyes again, and listened as the rumbling sounds were overlain with the spattering of raindrops hitting the compacted earth outside and overhead. The intensity of the storm built rapidly then, as if it knew she was awake. The lightning came more quickly, stabbing and battering the earth.

And the sound. Thunder now became separate crashes instead of a low continuous rumble. Raindrop patter became sibilant: the rush of real rain. Drops no longer struck earth — they joined deepening puddles. Puddles joined streams. Runoff generated a new coursing, flowing sound all its own. The storm was alive and rushing toward her sanctuary.

When it arrived, she could no longer lie still, listening. She leaped to her feet, eyes wide open, fully awake. She crossed the room amid lightning pulses so rapidly paced that each slice of her movements became a separate event, frozen stroboscopically, witnessed in isolation. She had one thought: to get out. But out was no better than in. As she reached the doorway, she was ankle-deep in water; the storm had pushed muddy, warm runoff up to the house. It flowed over her feet, along the sides of the house, then out through loose weave of the walls. The hair on her arms stood on end. Dense, falling rain obscured everything beyond the flattened area just in front of the doorway, in front her. The lightning shone like daylight on it, milliseconds at a time.

And then she was no longer alone.

An old man was there, outside, in the rain with his dog —a dog that looked more like a coyote. At first, they stood looking at the sky; she thought they might drown in the falling rain. Then they began to dance, slowly at first, shuffling, rhythmically walking around the clearing, to a tempo in the storm that only they heard.

The beat of the dance increased with the intensity of the storm. She heard a voice between the sound of the wind and rain and between the claps of thunder; she realized that the old man was chanting.

The blinding, clear illumination of the lightning flashes portrayed the dance of the old man and the coyote in freeze-frame still life. So compelling was each scene that Dana was unaware that the coyote had transformed. Now, dancing before her were two men. The lightning hit so frequently, now, that it was almost continuous, and she could see the dancers clearly. The second man appeared younger, and he was definitely larger—almost a giant by comparison. He looked to have been carved from the native stone of the mountains by a classical sculptor seeking to portray the physical aspect of a god.

The big man's movements followed the dance of the old man, mimicking them, at times mocking them. As she watched him, she knew he watched her. His eyes never sought hers, but she knew that he saw her in the doorway. She felt as though his dance was deliberately provocative, sensual, and directed toward her. She knew that the old man, too, danced for her benefit, but in a different way.

The storm began to move past. The intensity of the rain diminished. The wind eased. The frequency of the lightning slowed. She felt as though it would be all right to breathe again.

The dance also slowed. The big man caught her eye and smiled. In the next flash of lightning, the dance stopped, and the old man looked to her, waved. They had survived the storm together; they must celebrate. She was surrounded by the feeling that life exists at the sufferance of the forces of earth and sky. People should be joyful when life, having been challenged, is renewed.

The storm moved on further. In the now lazy lightning, in the now gently pattering rain, the old man and the coyote walked into the night. They were gone before she could move or speak.

❊   ❊   ❊

THOUGH DANA HAD come to the summer house alone, she hadn't been unobserved. Someone else had been there with her, even at the height of the storm.

Now, as it passed, the storm left the young man cold, wet, and wonderfully alive. He felt the renewing power of the rain; he felt energized, electrified. He had been cleansed, and he had taken the power of the storm for his own. It would be part of him forever.

His uncle had told him to allow no harm to come to the *Medigán* woman, but to avoid contact with her unless it was needed, then only as a last resort. After her arrival, he had marked in his mind places where he might see and not be seen. The best of them was just across the *a'ak* that ran next to the summer house, but he knew that he would have to leave his niche before the storm hit. It was the shortest linear distance from her, but rain in any quantity would fill the arroyo. He would be unable to reach her if he needed to act.

He settled into the cleft. The *Kui's* tap root had anchored the old mesquite tree for fifty years, until the bank of the wash had eroded back that far. Moving water scooped out the dirt and rock all the way around the thick root, leaving room enough for a man to stand or sit, directly opposite the summer house. The trunk had leaned and finally toppled half-way over in such a way that green, living branches shielded the pocket from view.

He had rested during the heat of the day, even taking catnaps of five or ten minutes while she was unpacking and preparing her meal. He had brought little to eat, preferring sparse trail food to a full pack. While she had cooked, he ate dried meat, corn meal he made into mush with a little water, and a prickly pear fruit; too much food makes one slow to think and slow to move. The tree, the *Kui*, provided a bubble of Mesquite sap and two dried seed pods for his dessert. He scattered the seeds in the bed of the wash, perhaps to spring to life downstream.

When the last warmth of the setting sun had left his face, he thought about moving, but he delayed, watching her. She had settled down in the clearing just in front of the summer house. Good, he thought, you can learn much about this place by being still and opening yourself to it.

She was not much to look at, he thought. *Too skinny. But maybe there was strength in her.*

He watched her counting the stars. Beans. Did she know that the Milky Way is white Muni beans that were scattered across the sky by the Immortals?

She tired of sitting, and moved into the house. He did not, and moved out of the niche, down the *a'ak* a few paces. He knelt in the moon-shadow of a greasewood, where he could see into the doorway, where he would be able to watch her sleep. Watching is a skill and an art. It must be learned and re-learned every time. It must be practiced with patience.

He moved when the clouds began moving quickly in their direction. He circled back, away from the summer house, then turned and walked slowly upstream away from the *vo'o,* parallel to the wash. At a safe distance, he crossed to the other side, and began walking back slowly.

Your prey doesn't become aware of you easily, he thought, *when you're walking away from them. Prey doesn't see slow movement. Prey doesn't look very far behind them. Prey will surprise you, though with what they do see. Always be careful. Always.*

His new place was hidden by brush, on a small hill overlooking the house. He could see in four directions, and he could see into the doorway. But in daylight, his form could have been noted by a careful observer; it was a position to be used in the night.

The storm didn't surprise him when it came. He had

watched it, too, as it swept up from Mexico along the trail that only the summer storms could see. He moved off the hill, not wishing to become a target for the lightning, and found cover in the lee of a few large rocks. The storms of summer were the life of the O'odham people. The O'odham danced every year to bring the storms, but that was earlier, when the fruit of the *Haʃan*, the saguaro, ripened. He wondered that this storm had come on so quickly, so late in the year.

It must be needed, he thought, as gentle rain began, whispering a warning of the storm to come.

The familiarity of the sudden storm was comforting to him. In the thunder, he heard drumming. In the lightning, he saw his whole family dancing. Memories of childhood summers surfaced in his mind, and the memories took control of his sight as his eyes sought to pierce the nearly impenetrable sheets of rain.

The memories stopped when he saw her in the door, and he again became only a watcher.

He sensed that she wanted to flee, but she saw that flight was not an option. *How will she react to the Power?* He wondered, *Will you run? Will you stand?* His glance followed her stare toward the *vo'o* in front of the house. And then he saw them.

There he saw his father, his mother and his two sisters returning home from the home of his Father's-Older-Brother after the wine ceremony. A version of himself as a boy followed far behind. The boy stopped to examine each stone, each leaf, to catalog how each had changed in the rain. He

117

measured his foot in his father's footprint, now filled with muddy water, and then measured his child's stride against that of a grown man. The boy looked up when lightning struck the hill, and the eyes of the child met the eyes of the man.

His next conscious thought was that the rain had stopped. It had only slackened, but it was so light that it didn't really count as rain, anymore.

I have survived again, he thought. He felt that in some way the storm had been meant to happen for him: to affirm his right to be in this place, to touch him with the power of the lightning.

❖ ❖ ❖

RETREATING INTO THE hut, exhausted by the power of the storm and the surrealism of the dancers, Dana found she could not fall back asleep, though the storm had taken most of the night. Dawn was only a few short hours away, along with the sun's heat and her ride home in the Sun Pony.

She sat up then moved outside, settling back to lean against the prickly wood just by the door. The pain may help me focus back on the physical world, she thought.

She watched the scene with new understanding. The natural movement, the dance, of each bush tree, and stone in her field of view had been taught to her by their behavior during the storm. The gentle wind now blowing diminished the movements, but the underlying pattern was there to see.

Except...

Some of the shadows moved out of tune with the whole. The wrong movements didn't come often, and they were always at the edge of her perception. But...

GET a GRIP on it, 'GUR-ull', she thought, imitating an O'odham drawl in her head. You're just too wrung-out to sit up in the middle of the night. Go lie down inside.

Still, she thought the shadows had looked like invading spiders from the dream world of the storm, and they seemed to be slowly making their way toward the hut. Let me wake up before they get here, she thought before closing her eyes in her exhausted state.

❖   ❖   ❖

THE YOUNG MAN watching her saw the moving shadows, too, but he knew they were not of the dream world. They moved slowly, sidling like shadow spiders, because they did not wish to be seen. They did not want to be seen because they had bad intentions.

He had to move before they reached the woman's hut. He used the *a'ak* as cover as best he could. Careful not to splash in the water that remained in the little arroyo from the rain, his pace was slow, slower than he wanted.

He rose up behind the hut in time to see a shadow easing toward, then into the open entrance on the opposite side. Moving as quickly as he dared, staying silent in the mud and storm debris, he entered the hut. In time, he thought.

Reaching out his arm he intercepted the rattlesnake strike intended for the sleeping woman. The rattlesnake head was at the end of an arm. The arm was clad in black and belonging to a crouched human attacker. The snake's extended fangs caught in the sleeve of his shirt, but stopped at the leather gauntlet he wore underneath. The snake head fell to the floor of the hut as the attacker dropped to his knees then rose again.

Their stances were inhibited by their proximity, but the young man and the invader moved quickly, with the self-assurance of practiced fighters. From somewhere, the black-clad attacker produced wooden *nunchakus* fashioned from unpolished ebony and black silken cords, and turned his attention to the young man. The young man could read his intentions as easily as the patterns of wind and water. It would appear that he and Dr. Gibbs had died together, battered to death in the sudden flood by rocks and debris. It would serve to send the same message as Dr. Gibbs' death by snakebite. The young man took his clasp-knife in hand.

He was used to working livestock, and the folding knife was sharp. Good fit in the hand; good for close quarters. Could be that a black shadow will wind up gelded here tonight, he thought.

The O'odham man had never fought like this before, though. Two swings of the *nunchakus*, and the knife was on the floor. So was he, holding his cheekbone where the stick had struck it hard, and trying to see through the stars that crowded his vision.

120

So fast and so silent had the action been that the girl had not stirred.

The invader raised his weapon for a killing blow, but found himself restrained. Two inhumanly large hands gripped his wrists, and the owner of those hands growled low, "Stop."

The attacker tried twisting, tried leveraging, tried feinting, tried rolling to free his wrists, but he had never fought an opponent that was carved from stone, as this one seemed to be.

"You try again, I will break them," the carved man said in a voice that rumbled like the storm's. "We wait. Outside."

After waking Dana, the young man took her outside as well. By this time, first morning light was waking the desert around them, and it allowed them to see the three men outside.

The invader was sitting cross-legged in front of the old man as the carved-stone man stood behind. The seated figure was dressed in traditional ninja-black silk. The fabric appeared to have been given a non-traditional treatment with stealth camo 'bots. It was difficult to focus on the shifting boundary of where the cloth ended and the rocky ground began. His hands were bound simply, but the Big Man held the loose end of the rope, and that seemed deterrent enough.

"You killed the other man, the security chief, using your snake head, why?" asked the young man.

The attacker answered with a sneer. "Your security chief was blocking us. We were attempting to make contact with Dr. Miguel through your systems. We needed you to know that we did it. That's why we chose snakebite."

"But why the artificial venom? You knew it would be discovered. Why keep going and try to harm this little one?" the young man indicated Dana.

"The first layer of our deceit gave you a cover story for the death of your employee: death by misadventure, as the British might say. We allowed you to discover that the snake venom was produced by one of our affiliates in Japan as a second layer. That would serve to warn you that a powerful enemy was behind the incursions—one best left alone lest you face mortal peril. As for why her? Ask her, she should know."

Dana interrupted, "You were the ones who came after the University's research, weren't you?"

"No," said the man. "We came after your research, and it just happened to be at the University. When we discovered your processor research, our staff concluded that your neural net processor experimentation was showing great potential. Our leadership thought it best to contain it by making a friendly takeover bid. Your university saw the wisdom of cooperating with us.

"These same tools identified the Center's neural net processor activity, though with much more difficulty. In fact, your job offer was one of the pointers that led us here. As before, our intrusion attempts here at the Center were the opening of 'negotiations', but this time with the O'odham. After your security chief defeated our attempts, we went one step farther.

"About a month ago, we approached your Center Director indirectly, through mutual friends in Shanghai—the ones he is currently visiting. Our offer was generous; we would assure both the O'odham and the Chinese unfettered cooperation of our development assets in Eurasia in exchange for a formal joint venture structure in certain research areas. While the Chinese agreed to these terms, Dr. Miguel did not. Our leadership concluded that the O'odham Center would never accept a formal joint research effort in the way the University had."

Almost as an aside, he continued, "The Center is well known for its proprietary attitude toward its research. Dr. Miguel has a reputation for being uncompromising and unyielding in negotiations. He gave you his 'great spoils' speech, I suppose." Fueled by indignation, the invader was now eager to talk. "You people are fools not to collaborate with anyone from the outside.

"So your security chief, and his replacement, here," he indicated Dr. Gibbs, "had to pay with their lives. It didn't matter whether she died from a snake's venom or the beating the storm would give her. You would know it was your enemy who reached out and took her life at will. Just as you would understand that we will reach out and take whatever else we want—regardless of your precautions."

"But you failed in your mission, here. We have you, and we will bring you to justice for your crimes," The young man said.

The attacker made a dismissive gesture. "Do you think I'd be so foolish as to speak plainly if I'd come here alone?"

"You mean them?" asked Coyote-man. He threw down

three black-sheathed swords and three hoods. "They're layin' down in a pile 'round back. Won't be gettin' up, though. Ever."

They all sat silently for several heartbeats. Then, solemnly, Dr. Miguel's nephew said, "We'll treat their remains with respect and bury them here in the manner our culture tells us is proper. We'll let you send their swords and belongings to their families when we take you back."

"That is very polite of you," said the attacker, "but I must decline. I must stay here with my team. I have failed them and failed in my mission; it is my duty to complete my obligation."

With that, he produced a knife that had been concealed in a pant leg. In one motion, he cut his bonds and plunged the blade into his abdomen at the correct spot and angle to begin ritual *seppku*. After the knife's final twist, he nodded to them and broke the capsule hidden in his tooth, administering his own coup de grace.

The Big Man and the young man had snapped into defensive postures when their prisoner had pulled the knife, but they couldn't react quickly enough to prevent his death. Now the four companions stared at his stilled form, even as the camo 'bots in his clothing tried to make it melt and flow into a background image.

They stared in shocked, silent disbelief. No one wanted to break the silence following the invader's death, but the silence grew painful and the two men eventually took him to rest with his fallen comrades.

"I don't even know your names," Dana said when they

124

were back together. "Though you all seem to know mine."

The old man spoke first. "'Round here we're real careful with names. To know a name is to have power. To know a person's true name is to have power over that person."

The young man said, "Among friends, we usually make up nicknames and use them instead of given names. We should do that now."

The big man said, "This one," nodding at Dana, "Independent Spirit. Acts alone. She's tough."

The young man suggested, "We can call her Spirit." And the others nodded in agreement.

Dana came back, "And you were the first to come to my rescue. I'd call you 'Defender'."

"At least it's not 'Shining Armor'," The young man joked back. "I'll take it if you just call me 'D'."

She continued, "And you, grandfather. You can only be Grandfather to me."

The old man corrected her, "I think the relationship you seek to name is, in our culture, Mother's Older Brother. I accept."

"How about me?" the big man asked.

Dana volunteered, "You look like a sculpture to me. A man cut from stone. How about 'Stone Man'?"

D countered, "My father told me a story about our village when grandfather was a boy.

"Every year, in the autumn, families would go to town and buy things for the children to get them ready for a new year at school. For most, there was never enough money to go around, and that meant the oldest boy and the oldest girl got new clothes and new shoes. Everyone else got hand-me-downs.

"One of the families had so many kids that the poor little guy at the end of the line had to make do with whatever was left. No matter what the color, no matter what the size, he had to take what clothes his mother said he could have.

"Usually, the least-shabby clothes came from the oldest of his older brothers. This little guy always seemed to have on pants that were two sizes too big for him. His whole village took to calling him 'Big Pants'.

"Well, Big Pants went on to finish school. Finish the U of A. He was the first O'odham elected to the U.S. Congress. In DC, they called him 'the Honorable...' but at home, everyone still called him 'Big Pants.'"

Turning to the big man, D said, "You, my bigger-than-life friend, are one fella that's gotta have big pants. I'd like to call you 'Big Pants' from now on."

"Big Pants," the big man rumbled. "I LIKE IT!"

Big Pants and D left to complete the funerary honors for the fallen invaders. Idly, D wondered how their deaths would be taken by their Zaibatsu. They had come to ensure their company's successful breach of the Center's defenses. To strike at their Center itself? To spy on their Chinese rivals? Maybe Uncle would know.

When they were alone, Spirit said, "Mother's Older Brother, this was your storm, wasn't it? You brought it so the four of us that would confront the dangers together."

Mother's Older Brother smiled slightly and said, "The world provides. In *Medigán,* you would say, 'Nature gives us all the resources we need.'"

"But..." she started, then stopped. Maybe some questions don't have answers; she thought, maybe some questions don't need answers.

After the invaders had been buried and the two men returned, Spirit and D drifted away from the others. They began to walk back to the pre-arranged pick-up point to wait for Tilly and the Sun Pony.

"I don't know how to say 'thank you' in the O'odham language", Spirit said quietly.

"You can't," D said. He saw her confusion and explained. "In our way of thinking, people always have a choice: doing what's right, or not doing what's right. When people choose to do the right thing, there's no need for thanks. It's just what they're supposed to do. No need for thanks, means no word for thanks.

"Sometimes though," he added, "In a situation like this, some people might say 'God will bless you for that.'"

Yes, Elder Brother—the old man—thought to himself, He will.

Big Pants just barked a laugh.

Spirit and D turned in time to see an old man and his dog walking away, heading to the place where the sun would set after blessing the still-cold desert with life-giving warmth.

Death

Benefits

by

Emily Baird

SK HADN'T MEANT to rescue the old woman or her groceries, but she had been taking so much time trying to carry the bags up the stairwell that he'd gotten impatient. SK knew he couldn't go back to play in his own stairwell—in the same building, but one door down—because the movers had the whole thing jammed with boxes and chairs and Bronte's soccer equipment and Danny's bookshelves and Milton's baseball bats. He couldn't play outside, because even though there wasn't any snow, it was way too cold out there. So if SK wanted to play in the stairwell, he realized he was just going to have to help the lady.

"Thank you for your help, young man."

"You're welcome." SK shifted the bags in his grip while the woman looked at him expectantly, "Ma'am," he added after that awkward second or two while the she peeled off her coat, scarf and gloves, and then carefully smoothed her hair—SK wondered if it might be a wig—back into place. SK's own coat still lay in a corner of the vestibule where he'd thrown it when he got too hot from running up and down during his gravity experiment. He would much rather have been out in the snow —he had so many questions about snow!—but there had been no snow yet. Not a flurry, not a flake, not flicker. Did snow flicker, SK wondered. He didn't know.

"If that home health aide really wanted to help out, he'd

go do the marketing for me, don't you think? Now, you just call me Miss Tonnie. That's my name, dear," she told him, shuffling carefully down her dark, lemon and pine-scented hall. "At church, all the boys and girls used to know me by Miss Tonnie."

Her apartment was almost identical to the one that SK and his family were currently moving into on the other side of the wall. But this one, SK could tell as he lugged the groceries after her, was smaller. Not too many people needed as many rooms as the Meyers-Coleson family did.

"The cans need to go down in that bottom cupboard, if you wouldn't mind, young man," Miss Tonnie told him as she carefully—and slowly—tucked a loaf of bread into a wooden breadbox. "Now then, I'm afraid you have me at a disadvantage," she told him, piercing him again with her expectant gaze.

"Ma'am," he said quietly, since that was pretty much the only way SK ever said anything. "What do you mean? Do you want me to help with putting these away, or not?"

"Oh child, I just mean that you know what to call me, but I don't know what to call you," her smile deepening the creases in her coffee-toned cheek. Her skin wasn't as dark as SK's, but SK had never met anyone whose skin was. Her gaze drifted away from him, as she studied the floor intently while moving to her table. After placing a few apples into a bowl, she lowered her long frame into a chair.

"Well, you can call me SK. That's what my family calls me."

"Esskay? Is that a family name? It's very handsome, of course," she told him as she switched her salt stained shoes for a pair of battered slippers that waited by the wall.

"Sort of is, and sort of not." SK paused because he wasn't sure how much she really wanted to know and how much she just really wanted someone to put her cans away. "It's short for Stephen King."

"Oh my goodness, no! Like that man with those scary stories? For a nice young man like you?" She laughed, more to herself though, while absently rubbing her knees.

SK opened her cabinet and began putting the cans away. It wasn't very hard because there wasn't much else in there. One can of French fried onions—like for that kind of green bean casserole that his sister Danny liked so much—a box of saltine crackers, a box of powdered milk and two cans of something called veg-all.

"I was sort of named for that writer guy because we all have writer names, but also I got my name from my biological dad. He was named Esteffan King." SK continued to read labels as he stacked the cans in neat rows. Peas, green beans, chicken soup, cream of mushroom soup—all with those plain white labels and just the words, no pictures. "But my name is Stephen King Meyers-Coleson. SK for short cause it sounds like Esteffan, and it's my first two initials."

Miss Tonnie was nodding as she listened to him, still rubbing, but mostly just her right leg now.

"Is powdered milk any good? Do you sprinkle it on things?" he asked her, curiosity getting the better of him.

"I wouldn't know, child. I've got the lactose intolerance. I always did prefer my tea sweet anyway."

"So why do you have so much in here?"

"Well now, that must be from when Walter was here last." Still she rubbed, but the smiles were gone. She looked far away now. SK wanted to ask her more questions, but Danny and Dad were always saying that he should try to figure things out on his own rather than asking other people and making them do the work. Who was Walter, he wanted to ask. When was he here last? Will he be coming back and wanting to have some powdered milk? Would he sprinkle it on something? How do you powder milk? You can't crush it up like pepper or wheat because it's liquid. Why was flour called flour and not powdered wheat?

"Oh, now where are my manners?" Miss Tonnie cried suddenly. SK looked up to see her wiping her right eye. "May I offer you some hospitality?" She rose slowly as she spoke, balanced against the teetery table, waiting for the last possible moment before putting her full weight on her legs. "Even though we've been having some warm weather for January, somehow I don't think it's warm enough for a glass of sweet tea, do you?" She moved toward her fridge, one hand clutching at the table's edge as she crossed the short distance.

Not sure how to tell her politely that he didn't like tea, SK just nodded.

"No indeed. In Chicago even a warm January is too cold for sweet tea. Just too cold..." her voice slowing to a trickle as she focused on her difficult journey across the kitchen until she stood by the counter across from SK. There, she paused, her hand wavering over a rainbow of canisters arrayed along the chipped tile counter top. "You seem a bit young for a coffee drinker, but perhaps a cup of cocoa would suit?"

"Yes, thank you, ma'am."

They drank their cocoa in Miss Tonnie's living room. Miss Tonnie led the way, even slower than before. She pressed her right hand against the wall, pushing herself forward bit by bit. So even though SK was being extra careful because he had two mugs of hot cocoa to carry down the hallway, he still had plenty of time to look at the pictures hanging just above the grey smudged trail that Miss Tonnie's hand followed. He looked particularly closely at one of them, because as she passed it, Miss Tonnie had brushed it with the trembling, ring-encrusted fingers of her free hand. He could see where the glass was blurry from being touched a lot.

The picture was very serious. The man's expression was a little bit fierce, SK thought. Instead of looking straight into the camera, he was looking at something farther away, something a little farther above. His hair was shaved so close that SK could see his skull gleaming beneath the brim of his white hat. There were medals and gold bits and buttons on his black coat and it looked very solemn.

"That's my baby," Miss Tonnie said as SK paused to look at the serious photo. "Such a brave boy, such a strong heart, my Walter."

SK nodded, because he didn't know what to say. Was

Walter her son, or her husband? Sometimes people used "baby" to talk about other people who weren't their kids. SK's mom never called him baby, even though he was the youngest, but she did sometimes call Dad baby.

In the living room, Miss Tonnie gestured to the coffee table while she settled herself into her couch. SK took his time putting down the cocoa because he knew it was important to pay attention to both mugs, and not forget the one in your left hand while you put down the one in your right hand. That's how he always did it, no matter what Bronte said about that time with Dad's computer and the chocolate milk.

"Well, Mr. Stephen King Meyers-Coleson, I believe that you are new to my building, aren't you?" Miss Tonnie asked him, settling into her place on the couch, pulling a corner of a blue and white fleece blanket over her slippered feet.

SK nodded, swallowing his cocoa. He liked that she remembered all of his name. Some people left parts out or got it wrong or, worst of all, called him Steve. "We just moved from California. There was supposed to be snow."

Miss Tonnie chuckled—a low throaty sound that made SK think of the organ at church. "Don't you worry, SK, there will be snow for you before the winter is out." She shook her head and raised her mug slowly, holding it with both hands. "I hope you don't mind, but I have been mighty curious about the goings on over there," Miss Tonnie told him, nodding her head toward the window on the far side of her living room.

The window, SK realized, looked right into the

sunroom of their new apartment. He could see lots of boxes and, in a little patch of clear space, the back of Bronte's head while she played mountain climbing Marbie. "I don't mean to intrude, but it helps keep my mind off things like death benefits. Benefits, I told that young man who calls himself my Casualty Assistance Calls Officer." Miss Tonnie shook her head. "Benefits are not something you get out of death. There are no benefits in the death of your son. Not for me. Not for any soldier's mama."

"Been a...fits?" SK asked, trying to figure the word for himself.

"There's nothing that fits about death, now, is there? You can't put a price on the life of a child. I didn't want their money six months ago, and I don't want it now."

"No ma'am," SK answered, hoping to reassure her. He still wasn't sure what a benefit was, but he was pretty sure that Miss Tonnie was telling him that her son was dead. SK knew about soldiers dying from reading some of Dad's blogs.

Abruptly changing the subject, Miss Tonnie gestured with her mug toward Bronte. "And who is that, right there?"

"That's my sister, Bronte. She's eight and she's not supposed to be playing on the boxes."

"No?"

"No. Mom said that the moving boxes were not toys and we cannot play on them because she didn't want us getting crushed by falling cartons of books, or breaking all our dishes if we were the ones falling. I went out to play on the stairs. But the movers kept needing to get by and one of them said some really bad things when my super-bouncy-power ball gravity tester hit him on the ear."

"There's never any call for using bad words when there are so many good words in the world. That's what I always say."

"What are good words for getting hit in the ear?" SK asked, tilting his head in thought, while Miss Tonnie watched him, smiling into her mug. "You could say 'ow.' But is 'ow' a word?" he wondered.

"I don't know that it is. It certainly isn't a very interesting word, even if it is, though, is it?"

They sipped their cocoa silently together for a few moments, accompanied by the radiator's subtle clicking and long-winded hisses, while SK thought about words for getting hit in the ear with a super bouncy power ball. Miss Tonnie, he realized after a moment, was still watching Bronte.

Now Bronte was making Marbie leap from box to box, circling around the room. In four more box tops, SK realized, Bronte would be looking back at them through the window. SK couldn't think of any way that it would be good if Bronte saw him. There was no way that Bronte wouldn't tell Mom and Dad, and there was no way that Mom and Dad wouldn't get mad at him for going into the apartment of someone he didn't know.

"I should probably go," he said already moving into the hallway and out of the window sightline. "I'll just put this in the kitchen. Thank you for the cocoa, Miss Tonnie."

"Well, SK Meyers-Coleson, I would like to thank you

for being my guest this afternoon. It has been a pleasure to have your company. You must be sure to stop by again soon. Not too many people come visiting anymore. That home aid worker hardly even counts. Always wanting to help out, he says. Oh, I'll cash that for you Mrs. Huguley, he says. But do something useful, like helping with the grocery shopping? That's not allowed by the union, he says."

"I wouldn't want to get in the way—" SK began.

Miss Tonnie shook her head and favored him with a watery smile, "It's good to have something to look forward too. It's a welcome change."

SK shook her hand before he left, because he felt like he had to do something to make sure that she didn't get up to see him to the door. Her heavy rings and thin fingers were cold in his cocoa-warmed palm. Hugging would have been weird when he'd just met her, he thought, but later, after it was all over, he wished he'd hugged her anyway.

❖   ❖   ❖

"SK, Mom said to stop watching TV!" SK could see Danny reflected in the sunroom window, standing behind him with her hands on her hips.

"No, Mom said to turn off the TV, and I did," SK told her, not bothering to turn around from where he leaned his chin against the back of the couch. With his knees on the cushions, and his nose to the window, he could see into Miss

Tonnie's living room, where her huge TV flickered merrily from its perch high on top of a tall, narrow bookcase. A couple of days ago Miss Tonnie noticed that he liked to watch her TV through the window. She'd changed the channels until he nodded, letting him see almost all of the Mythbusters where they blew up the water heater. SK loved that one. Today they were watching Animal Planet.

Danny kneeled on the couch next to him, peering through the window. "Don't you hate that you can't hear it?"

"No." There were like a million kittens, and they were getting really crazy, ripping up a bean-bag chair. It really didn't need a lot of talking. "I hate that there's no snow. It's too cold to go outside, but there's no snow. Chicago sucks." Now someone had given the kittens a tower of toilet paper rolls to climb and demolish. The flying fluff was more snowy than anything he'd seen outside.

"It's supposed to snow tomorrow night. I saw it on the news," Danny rested her chin on the back of the couch like SK. "Do you think she minds you watching? I mean, like, looking in her window?"

"No. She smiles when she sees me." One of the kittens made it to the top of the toilet paper pile, only to have the roll under him, well, roll under him. SK giggled.

"How can you tell she's smiling when her back's to the window?" Danny asked. "Did you see her smile today?"

SK scowled. "No. But I know she doesn't mind. Sometimes she changes during commercials, but she only turns to kid channels. See!" SK tapped the window, close enough that his breath threatened to fog out his view of the TV next door. "She's changing the channels now!"

"That's not a kids' channel," Danny noted, as Miss Tonnie's TV filled up with black and white static, then flickered back to the commercials, then back to the static.

"Do you think her TV's broken?" SK asked absently, mesmerized by the dance of color and static alternating on the screen across the way. Color, static, color, static, color, static; it flipped with dizzying speed. Then slowly, lingering a second or two with each channel; color...beat, static...beat, color...beat, static...beat, color...beat, static...beat. Then fast again. The changes made SK's eyes squint up. "It's like something's wrong with the TV, or something. I don't like watching it."

"I don't think that guy likes you watching it, either," Danny said, just before popping her head down, out of the window's line of sight.

Even if SK had had time to move, he was too frozen by shock to respond. Because just as Danny had spoken, a white figure had crossed through Miss Tonnie's living room, and dropped the blinds. SK didn't scream. It couldn't have been a scream, because all his muscles clenched up, making his throat and face so tight that nothing like a scream could ever have made it passed his lips. But yah, he did make a choking, kind of whimpering noise.

"SK, are you all right?" Danny asked, slowly rising from where she had collapsed on the cushions. SK shook his head, because he was not all right, or even a little bit right.

Miss Tonnie hadn't even turned to look at the person

walking through her apartment. She hadn't even looked away from the TV. She had just stayed right there on the couch, with her legs up, all covered with her blanket, just like she'd been all day. And yesterday. It was like she didn't think there was anyone there with her.

"You saw him?" he asked his sister, still staring at the covered window, "You saw, like, a person?" SK could see Danny's reflection now, nodding. "But she didn't move," SK said, mostly to himself, "It was like he wasn't there."

"There was something there. Someone."

"What did he look like?"

"I don't know. A guy." Danny shrugged behind him.

"You said he looked like he didn't want me watching, so you saw his face. What did he look like? Black, brown, grey, green-what?" SK flipped around on the couch to face his sister. "You're the one who remembered that Mrs. Packard had gold rimmed glasses that time that she lost them at the pool, so come on Danny. What did you see?"

Danny looked at him with her mouth all puckered up for a moment before she sighed and flopped down on the couch next to him. "At first I thought he was white. But he was wearing white and, really, he seemed more like a black guy, but faded or something. Not white or blond, just pale. His eyes were weird. They were this weird yellow color." Danny paused, chewing her lip. "He was pretty creepy, I guess, sort of like a ghost. A ghost man."

SK nodded. He didn't need Danny to tell him the guy was creepy. That much he had seen for himself.

❖   ❖   ❖

IT WASN'T UNTIL after school the next day that SK was able to convince one of his siblings to go next door with him, so he could check on Miss Tonnie. The blinds had been down when he'd checked before school and right when he got home, so as soon as he had a chance, he asked Milton to play catch. Milton never, ever said no to catch. And if Milton didn't know that it hadn't really been an accident when SK threw one of Milton's baseballs onto Miss Tonnie's sun porch, then that would never hurt him. Miss Tonnie's porch didn't have any screens or glass windows like most of the other apartments, so pitching the ball in there hadn't been too hard. Keeping Milton from squashing him long enough to explain that they could go ask for it back from the lady that lived there? That had been much harder.

"Come on, it didn't break anything, so she won't be mad!"

"Damn it, SK, if Mom finds out we even almost broke somebody's window, she is going to bench me until high school and then I won't even have a shot at the minors! There's no way I'd get off easy like you did with the chocolate milk."

SK grimaced, but otherwise ignored his big brother. Tucking his glove under his arm, he headed for Miss Tonnie's stairwell. Milton would follow him.

"And seriously, you have got to learn control. I'd kill for an arm like yours," Milton muttered, following behind just like

SK knew he would. "And the name. God, Milton. Do you know how many Miltons have made it to the Bigs?"

SK didn't answer. He knew he didn't have to. They crossed through the entryway where the mailboxes were, skirting a few flyers that someone had scattered across the tile to absorb some long dried up puddle.

"Three. Eric Milton, Larry Milton, and God help me, Milton Bradley. That's a hole that's hard to hit out of."

SK didn't mean to roll his eyes, but it wasn't like he hadn't heard all this before.

By now they were half way up the stairs, thanks to some thoughtful neighbor who'd left a catalogue jammed in the inner door to keep it from locking. That's how SK got in last time too. The same scrubbed, grinning kids splashed each other in their tie-died rash guards on the cover—but the smiles and colors had wrinkled from the cold and their limbs were crumpled where the pages were wedged into a permanent doorstop. SK was glad he had Milton with him. Bronte would have yanked the catalogue out without a second thought. She hated anything that didn't follow the rules, once she understood whatever rules there were.

When he got to Miss Tonnie's door, SK was surprised by his nervousness. He knew Miss Tonnie would be glad to see him. He knew she wouldn't mind about the ball on her porch. She'd probably even be glad for a chance to visit. But standing there, in front of that big, dark slab of wood, all SK could think about was the figure in white he'd seen flicker so quickly through Miss Tonnie's living room.

If there really had been a person with Miss Tonnie, she'd have been talking to them. SK knew that she was polite like that. But if there hadn't been a person, then what had he and Danny seen? SK's hand shook a little bit as he raised it to knock. Milton beat him to it, though.

"Hello," Milton called, in between bursts of loud, jarring knocking. Pausing, Milton let his hand fall, shifting his mitt to the other side. "We should have checked the mailbox downstairs for her name," he said. "It doesn't seem like anyone's here—"

The door flew open in front of them, filled by the white clad figure of a man. The ghost man. He looked—at least as far as SK could tell—very real and very creepy and very mad. It could have been the way his features and his skin didn't quite seem to match. Or maybe it was the stale, bitter stench that wafted off him—like old cigarettes and rotting mushrooms. But it was probably because of his weird yellow eyes. SK told himself that the man couldn't help what color his eyes were or how weird they looked. Maybe he was mad because so many people thought he looked creepy because of his eyes and there really wasn't anything he could do about that. Well, he could have worn contacts, but SK didn't blame the man for not wanting to put little plastic cups on his eyes. Talk about creepy and gross.

"What?" the man growled at them, and SK realized that neither he nor Milton had said anything.

"I'm sorry, sir," Milton began before SK could figure out what to say, "but my brother threw our ball onto the —"

"The hell you say," the man sneered at Milton, glancing between Milton's tousled red hair, glasses and freckles and SK's pattern-shaved head and shining black skin. SK could feel Milton tense up next to him. Of all of them, Milton was the one who hated it the most when people were rude about them being family. SK worried that Milton might ask the man at the door if he was a card carrying member of the idiot party, like he had that time with Father Greeley. SK didn't think that would help him find out what was going on with Miss Tonnie.

"I'm adopted," Milton lied, staring the creepy ghost man down.

SK peered under the man's rigid arm, scrutinizing the apartment's hallway. "Is Miss Tonnie home?" he asked, his words falling between them like birds stunned to the ground after flying into a window. The man continued to stare back at Milton, the gap between his body and the door giving SK a glimpse of fluttering blue and white — Miss Tonnie's blanket. It flicked in and out view down the hall behind Ghostman's back. Like a handkerchief, or a signal flag, the blue and white fleece leapt in and out of sight at the corner of the hallway, just inches from where SK knew the living room couch was.

"And I don't give a fuck. Not about you, your brother or your fucking ball." And the door slammed shut in their faces.

Milton's eyes narrowed and his mouth screwed up in that way that made him look just like Danny. "What a jerk! Does he even live here?"

SK shrugged.

"Come on, let's go home and type up a really scary looking legal note about seizure of property."

SK didn't think that the door would open again, even if he knocked, but he hesitated to follow Milton down the stairs just yet. He didn't really know what to do, but he was filled — head to toe, brimming like how Bronte always filled her soda cups at the movie theater self-serve — with a feeling that he had to do something. Miss Tonnie had been sending him a signal. He was sure.

"Come on, SK," Milton called from the landing. Sighing, SK turned to follow.

Just as they got to the final flight, there was a loud thud and smashing sound from out front. Then the distinctive wail of a car alarm jarred through their skin. Milton's face paled, his freckles standing out. He gasped out a really bad word and sprinted down the remaining stairs. SK had a pretty good idea what he'd see when he got outside, and he didn't really want to hurry out to see it. And if he committed a federal offense after Milton had already left the building, then that meant that Milton couldn't get blamed too. SK hoped so because he really didn't want to Milton to get in any more trouble than he already would be when mom saw where his baseball wound up.

❊ ❊ ❊

"So TELL ME, in your own words, Milton, how your baseball wound up in the minivan's windshield. And take some green beans."

Milton accepted the bowl from his mother, deposited the required beans and passed it to SK. SK took some too, but he actually liked green beans, especially when covered in Dad's Thai peanut sauce. SK really wanted to tell Mom in his own words how the ball had gotten there, but he wasn't sure he'd get a turn. The baseball was Milton's, which meant that it was Milton's responsibility. SK knew that responsibility meant that you took care of something and that you made sure that it didn't get hurt—like how SK packed all his own fossils and rocks just to make sure that none of them got lost, or broken or accidentally mixed in with Danny's beach stone collection. Miss Tonnie wasn't his, not like a baseball or a fossil could be, but he still had a feeling that she might be his responsibility. No one else seemed to be thinking of her that way.

While Milton launched into his story—which relied heavily on the early career statistics of first baseman Bill Buckner for some reason clear only to Milton—SK stewed in worry. From his seat at the table, he could see into the sunroom and had a perfect view of the window that looked into Miss Tonnie's living room. Unlike every other night since they moved in, tonight he didn't see Miss Tonnie settling in for some Wheel of Fortune and a mug of soup. Tonight, he could only see thin scraps of icy blue light cutting through the infinitesimal slits of Miss Tonnie's closed blinds.

"SK? Mothership to SK." Mom's voice broke into his worried contemplation. The green beans were cold on his plate, sadly stranded in the congealed peanut sauce. "Do you have anything to add?" One side of Mom's mouth twitched as she and Dad exchanged one of their looks.

SK always had something to add. There were always questions someone didn't ask or answers that needed more questions to make sense. But he hadn't been listening, so he wasn't sure what needed asking. And he knew that asking to know what needed asking was probably not a good idea. Glancing up from his meal, SK looked at his family while they, in turn, studied him. Dad was packing up a couple of servings to freeze for Mom's lunches. Milton was plowing his way through a pile of rice and peanut sauce while expertly excavating each and every bean. Mom had her head tilted, looking at him the way she sometimes looked at the stuff she read for work, when it needed figuring out. Bronte—well, Bronte looked up at him and grinned, like usual. Last of all, he caught Danny's concerned gaze and raised his eyebrow. Danny silently mouthed a single word. Danny didn't have anything to apologize for, so it took him a minute to figure out why she had said sorry.

"SK?" Mom prompted.

Putting his fork down, SK met his parents' eyes steadily. "We should go apologize."

Mom and Dad exchanged a look while Milton bristled. "We should apologize for that jerk throwing our ball into our windshield? That is messed up, SK!" his brother threw at him from across the table.

"We should go apologize," he continued, "and we should check on the lady that lives there. To make sure she's okay."

"The ball didn't even go inside! Of course she's okay!" Milton choked the words out, getting a little red in his haste to swallow and defend himself. Dad paused on his way back to the kitchen to pat Milton on the back, attempting to soothe the subsequent coughing.

Mom smiled at SK. "That's a nice idea, SK. I'm sure the woman's all right, Milton. But that's very considerate of you to think of her, SK. It's a little late tonight, but I don't have office hours tomorrow afternoon, so we can go over after school."

"And we have to speak with her. We have to tell her we're sorry in person," SK insisted.

"I can certainly understand your reticence to confront the gentleman whose response appeared so inappropriate, but I think it's important that you consider how important it is to diffuse that enmity." SK didn't know a lot of those words, but even though he wasn't entirely sure what Mom had said, he was pretty sure he didn't like it. He could tell that Bronte certainly hadn't.

"You said no more big words during family talk!" Bronte told Mom, scowling. "You said you wouldn't talk about legal stuff or use words that were too big for me to handle, and —" she continued, showing every sign of a potential melt down, "I'm tired of baseball stories," she shot at Milton.

Ignoring Bronte's interruption—which was really the only way he thought anything got done in their family—SK continued his worrying out loud. "The weird thing is, she didn't open the door or at least come into the hallway. Because she's lonely."

"How would you know she's lonely?" blurted Bronte, pointing her fork at him.

SK hated it when Bronte poked holes in anything he said, just because she could. And you could never get mad at her in front of Mom and Dad, because Mom and Dad were always so happy when she 'displayed her unexpected cognitive capacity.' He gave his sister a sideways glare through slitted eyes, but didn't let her stop his thought process. "Anyone would be curious about someone at their door. And she's all the way up there on the third floor. Not many people come by, I bet."

"I don't see how she'd be too lonely, living there with her son like she does," Mom smiled at him, reassuringly.

"Her son?" How could Mom have talked to Miss Tonnie's son? He was dead!

"The young man at the door with the bad aim."

SK wasn't really sure how to proceed without admitting he'd been in Miss Tonnie's apartment. "How do you know he was the lady's son? What if she let him in because she was lonely or needed help and it turned out he was a bad guy?"

Mom raised an eyebrow at him, "SK, grownups know better than to let strangers into their homes. Just like you kids know better than to talk to strangers or enter strangers' homes." She smiled at each of them.

SK swallowed the guilt that burned in his throat. "What if he tricked her? Bad guys trick people! Or what if she forgot about strangers? People forget things they're supposed to remember, sometimes," he finished, weakly.

"He said he was her son, SK. He introduced himself to me out front this morning, said that he and his mother lived in 3C and welcomed us to the building. He was very well spoken and polite. And while I don't know he's the same person, he certainly fits the physical description given by you and Milton. Besides, SK," Mom continued, "the woman who lives there certainly isn't going to let a stranger into her apartment, now is she?"

If SK told her that yes, she would let a stranger into her apartment, then everyone would want to know how SK knew that. And if he told them how he knew that, then he would get in trouble. Probably big trouble. Bigger than chocolate milk trouble. Because everyone knew that strangers were a much bigger deal than spilled milk. So SK just nodded and asked to be excused from the table.

❀   ❀   ❀

"PLEASE DANNY, it won't be any of the websites we're not supposed to go to!" SK begged his sister after he'd tracked her to Dad's office where the computer was.

Danny scowled at him from over the top of the computer screen. "I actually have homework, SK. And I only get forty-five minutes on the computer before it's Milton's turn."

"Please? You know Milton will never let me. Please,

Danny? Please, please with sugar on it? I'll help you with your homework," he offered.

Danny scoffed at him, but she was smiling on one side of her mouth. "Ten minutes, that's it SK. If you don't find what you need in ten minutes —"

"Will you type for me? It'll go faster that way..." SK let his voice trail off, watching Danny's face closely. Elation filled him as the other side of his sister's mouth rose, completing her reluctant smile. "Just try Google, first, okay?" SK asked as he dug into his cargo pocket for the folded wad of papers he had stashed there earlier in the day. "We're looking for a Walter Booker," SK paused, unfolding the paper from the envelope to read, "Huguley," spelling it out, letter by letter, for Danny's fingers to type.

It wasn't the first link, or the second or the third. It was way down the list, after some stuff about genealogy and a bunch of reviews for Huguley's Books somewhere in Georgia. But there it was. SK pointed silently at the screen, and pulled his chair closer as Danny clicked on the link for the Chicago Tribune obituary page.

August 3, 2012 Chief Master Sergeant Walter Booker Huguley, U.S.M.C, age 44, beloved son of Antoniella and the late MGySgt (Ret.) Booker W. Huguley of Chicago, of wounds sustained when enemy forces attacked his unit in Helmand province, Afghanistan. CMSgt Huguley was a graduate of the University Lab School and received his Civil Engineering degree from the University Illinois at Champagne-Urbana.

Following a decade in the private sector, Walter enlisted in the Marine Corps, fulfilling a lifelong dream to follow in his father's footsteps. In lieu of flowers, donations may be made to Semper Fi Fund.

There was a picture with the article; a picture that SK recognized. It was smaller and there were no finger smudges on it, but SK knew it was the serious picture from Miss Tonnie's wall.

"Who's that?" his sister asked, "And why do you have someone's mail?"

"That's Miss Tonnie's son."

"Miss Tonnie?"

"She's the lady next door. And this is her mail. Her mailbox is all bent and doesn't close all the way like it should." SK laid the envelope next to the keyboard and smoothed the letter out over it. "Can you tell what it's about?"

"SK! Taking people's mail is a big deal! It's a big, big deal!"

SK nodded. He knew that. He knew that stuff in mailboxes was protected by Federal law. With a mom like theirs, it was pretty hard not to know things like that.

"Why would you do that?" his sister demanded.

"Remember move-in day when I said I played in the stairwell?" Danny nodded, tilting her head to meet SK's lowered eyes. "It wasn't our stairwell. It was the one next door. That's where I met Miss Tonnie. That's how I know her name and that's how I know that this," SK jabbed his finger at the picture on the screen, "was her son and not Ghostman."

"Okay," Danny said slowly, "so you know her name and you know that her son—" Danny glanced quickly at the article, "—Walter is dead. That doesn't mean that the guy we saw, the ghost man, wasn't her son too."

"But that guy doesn't look like Miss Tonnie, or like this picture that we know is her son!"

"Really, SK? Seriously?" Danny held up a hunk of her thick, blond hair with one hand and polished her little brother's nubby head with the other. "Families should be what you make with love, not what—"

"Not what you get stuck with because you don't open your heart," he finished with her. SK sighed. "I know that Danny. But just like I know that you're my sister, I know that Ghostman isn't Miss Tonnie's son. He's just not." SK reached around his sister's arm to click the back button on the computer. The list of Walters flashed back on the screen. Absently, SK rolled the mouse around on the desk, watching the little arrow turn into a pointing fingered glove, then back; glove, arrow, glove, arrow. Danny ignored him, engrossed in the letter SK had taken from Miss Tonnie's mailbox that afternoon.

"So you think your Miss Tonnie, the TV lady, is the same as this Antoniella Huguley?" Danny asked. SK nodded, not bothering to look up. "This letter is from the government and it says that she's supposed to have gotten a check for one hundred thousand dollars." Danny's eyes were wide.

"That's a lot, right? A lot in real money, to a grown up, right?" SK didn't quite know how to ask his question, but

Danny usually knew what he meant.

Danny nodded. "It's for something called a death benefit. And yeah, it's a lot."

"Is it so much that someone would want to steal it?"

"Probably. If they were the sort of person who steals things."

"But if Ghostman was just there to steal the money, why would he still be there? Why would he say he was her son? He could take her money and run down the stairs. She's real slow, so she wouldn't be able to catch him."

Danny shook her head. "Checks don't work like that, SK. People have to sign them and take them to the bank."

"What if she didn't sign it? Does that mean he can't steal it?"

"Look SK, I don't like this ghost man guy any more than you do," Danny told him, "but he's probably her son. Why would he lie?"

"To get a hundred or thousand or whatever dollars, that's why!" SK thumped the desk for emphasis, his knuckles whacking the mouse. The monitor washed over in white, then a photo appeared: the serious picture. Bit by bit, scraps of text loaded onto the page. It was another obituary, this one from the Sun Times.

On August 3, 2012, Chief Master Sergeant Walter Booker Huguley lost his life during a combat exchange with enemy forces in Afghanistan. A Chicago native, born and raised in Hyde Park, Walter was a graduate of the University Lab School and an engineering major at the University of

Illinois at Champagne-Urbana. The only son of Walter and Antoniella Huguley, longtime members of Liberty Baptist Church, CMSgt Huguley is survived by his mother, Antoniella.

SK stared at the words 'only son,' frozen on the screen. Behind them, SK imagined he saw the corner of a blue and white fleece blanket, flickering in and out of sight. Either the man next door was lying, or, if he really was Miss Tonnie's son, then he really was a ghost.

❖ ❖ ❖

SK COULD FEEL the heat of his brother's gaze on the back of his neck the whole way up to Miss Tonnie's apartment that next afternoon.

"I don't. See. Why we. Have to. Do this," Milton hissed between his gritted teeth with each mounted stair. Mom didn't hear him, but Milton was the least of SK's worries. At the door, Mom paused a moment before knocking, and SK carefully dried his sweaty palm before reaching into his pocket to grip his super-bouncy power-ball gravity-tester. SK hoped the door opened soon—before he lost his nerve and before his hand got all sweaty again and made the ball all slippery.

SK didn't know if it was because Mom knew how to knock like a grownup, or if it was because Ghostman had seen them walking over from their own stairwell, but the door opened almost right away, washing the landing with cold, cold air. Under his coat, Ghostman wore the same kind of clothes he'd worn yesterday—like people on hospital shows—but today they were blue and not white. He didn't glower, like yesterday, and he even seemed kind of polite when he said hello. But he still stank.

SK was glad he was ready with his plan, because almost as soon as the door opened, Ghostman sidled out into the landing and started to pull the door closed behind him. With skill born of many, many hours of super-bouncy power-ball gravity-testing experiments, SK whipped his hand from his pocket, flinging his ball in a wide and seemingly wild arc through the landing. When the ball bounced behind him and ricocheted off the walls before zigzagging full throttle through Miss Tonnie's open door, SK wore an expression of surprise and confusion.

"I'm sorry, I'm sorry," he insisted, rushing after his plastic accomplice before there was time to stop him.

Luckily the ball had angled toward the living room at the front of the apartment, rather than the back. And luckily, Mom was in the doorway with Ghostman, where SK could hear her apologizing in her competent, adult way for SK's awkwardness. Ghostman couldn't follow SK down the hall to the living room without SK's mom coming right behind. A little smile crept onto his face as SK scurried to the living room. The smile dropped when he saw Miss Tonnie.

It wasn't as bad as he'd imagined, not at first glance. Miss Tonnie wasn't tied up, or handcuffed to a chair, or gagged with socks and duct tape, or blindfolded. But any relief SK might have felt drained away in the horror of what he did see.

Miss Tonnie was only partially on the couch, and as SK watched, she struggled, one arm pulling on the couch frame and one leg pushing against the floor, vainly trying to get up. Or down. SK couldn't even tell which way she was trying to go. She wasn't wearing one of her typical, neat pantsuits. Instead she wore some kind of old fashioned nightgown; the pink and green flowered material torn and stained, the remains of one lace trimmed sleeve hanging in limp tatters against an equally limp and useless arm. Her fingers were all bare, and somehow that seemed even more obscene to SK's eyes than the sight of Miss Tonnie's legs splayed across the cushions. The material of her gown bunched around her waist, everything from her belly on down exposed to the cold. And it was cold. Very, very cold.

"Miss Tonnie?" SK whispered, as he circled around to see her face, his ball rolling forgotten across the floor. "Miss Tonnie?" Questions ripped through SK's mind, twice as many and twice as fast as usual, "Miss Tonnie, what happened?" The rest of his questions died on his lips. Miss Tonnie's right side, her arm and her leg, were flaccid and motionless, even as her left side gripped and strained against the couch.

Her wig was gone, leaving wisps of grey and white springing at odd angles from her skull, framing a face made both older and more vulnerable by an array of bruises. The left side of her mouth constricted and stretched while the right side hung, unmoving, from her jaw. She was making noises, SK realized, like she was trying to talk. With only half her mouth working, though, the noises failed to resolve into speech. The worst part was her eyes. The left rolled strangely, seeming to look anywhere but at SK. The right, however, pierced him — begging and desperate — while tears rolled down her distended, swollen cheek.

For once SK was glad that he was strong. Without a thought for the ghost man at the door, SK crossed the few steps to Miss Tonnie's side and helped her settle back on couch. He lifted the blanket, which sprawled on the floor, to cover her. There was no time to do more, even if he'd had any idea of what to do, before the sound of Ghostman's voice from the hallway brought SK to attention. He saw Miss Tonnie's good eye close, as if in defeat.

"Well now, aren't you nice for helping my momma," Ghostman exclaimed heartily as he entered the room, followed closely by SK's mom. "She's been having such trouble lately, haven't you Momma?" he asked, placing a proprietary grip on Miss Tonnie's shoulder and neck. "Just look what she did to her sleeve. Got it caught in the radiator."

Nausea roiled through SK's gut as Ghostman shook his head, turning to confide in SK's mom, his body preventing Mom from entering the room while his hand kept Miss Tonnie from turning her head. "It's hard being a parent to your parent, ain't that right? Just this morning she somehow got it into her head that the radiators needed cleaning, or draining. Really, God knows what she was thinking. She went around turning them all off, got her sleeve all torn and her nightdress all nasty." Ghostman reached around for the blanket, pushing himself between SK and the old woman. "She got to be more careful, or she might catch her death," he finished, tucking the fleece tightly around Miss Tonnie's now slack form.

Miss Tonnie's noises were quieter now, but somehow they seemed to be all that SK could hear. And even if he couldn't hear any words, SK knew exactly what Miss Tonnie was saying. He backed away from her, and from Ghostman, retreating toward the hallway. Mom hadn't budged from her position at the entrance to the living room, so SK quietly backed up against the window, out of the way and unnoticed, his hands busy behind him. SK could see that Mom's every muscle was tense and her jaw was set in her professional, I'm-a-lawyer-you-can't-fool-me-young-man mode. Her eyes narrowed momentarily, but then she nodded and broke into a smile.

"Oh my goodness, yes. Being a caregiver really is a full time job. But that's what we do for our family, isn't it?" She pulled SK up close to her in a mama bear hug as if to illustrate, before all but shoving him down the hallway toward the door. "Again, Mr. Huguley, we are so sorry for the trouble the boys caused with their ball-balls. Our apologies," she smiled, flicking a little half wave at him from the doorway. Still facing the door, she gestured for Milton—who'd waited the whole time in the hallway—and SK to get started down the stairs. She didn't turn to join them until the door was closed.

SK thought it would have been funny, if anything about any of this could be funny, that it was Mom who hissed curses and made muttered comments under her breath the whole way back to their apartment. "Must. Find out. About. Illinois.

Conservatorship. Laws," was the only bit that SK could hear. He didn't know what it meant exactly, but he wondered if mom might be on his side now.

It was too bad, then, that neither she nor Dad were home that night, when SK learned how bad things really were.

❅   ❅   ❅

"YOU ROLLED TWICE!" Bronte yelled, flinging Marbie, with very poor aim, at SK from across the dining room table. Always game for playing catch, Milton neatly fielded the doll before it impaled SK in the eye with a pointy-footed plastic leg.

"Did not!" SK shot back, even as he saw Danny nodding her confirmation of Bronte's assertion.

"Cheater!" Bronte yelled, scrambling over Danny in her effort to get around the table. SK ducked under the table and scooted across the floor to the other side, hoping that Milton and Danny would get her calmed down before she started kicking things at him.

Scrambling up from the floor, SK hovered near Danny. "I'm sorry, Bronte. I didn't mean to roll twice. I wasn't cheating, honest."

Bronte, Marbie back in her folded arms, narrowed her eyes at him. "That's what cheaters say."

"I'm sorry, I didn't mean to. Do you want two rolls?"

"No." Bronte sat down in SK's vacated chair with a finality that made it clear to everyone that she, at least, was done playing that evening's board game. "I want to know how you can forget that you just took a turn, like, two seconds ago."

SK chewed his lip, debating with himself about how much he could tell, even if Mom and Dad were out of the apartment at some faculty party thing. Milton and Danny joined Bronte at the table, all three watching him with varying degrees of interest or suspicion.

"Okay," he let out with a release of air, "Something's really, really wrong with Miss Tonnie. I keep checking her window to see if I can see anything."

"Who's Miss Tonnie?" Milton asked, craning his head around to look where SK was pointing. "That lady next door? We never even saw her. How do you know her name?"

Bronte turned around in her chair and squinted at the sunroom. "What window? The sunroom window?"

"Not the window on our side," Danny told her sister, leading the way into the sunroom and lifting the curtains aside to point. "The window of the apartment on the other side of the gap, right there. SK and I got her name from her mail—her mailbox." Listening as Danny spoke, Bronte crossed the room and opened the curtains the rest of the way. Moving to let Bronte see better, Danny added, "Google said that her only son died six months ago."

Milton shook his head, as he followed them into the sunroom, turning off the apartment lights as he came. "The internet isn't always right, Danny." With darkness behind them, they could see the pale wash of the streetlight below, and pick out the details of the stone and brick window ledge opposite them.

Bronte stared through the glass, concentrating on the other window with her trademark ferocity. "I don't see anyone. I don't see anything. Just the light flickering from the TV. Those broken blinds are in the way."

"I know," SK said as he came up from behind to join them. "That's the problem. You can't tell if she's okay or not." He knelt up on the couch with his sisters. "I tried to bend some of the slats back when I was in there today, but I didn't get enough of them. It's too far away to see anything."

Bronte sat up with a jerk. "You could use Milton's binoculars!" she crowed.

Behind them, Milton shook his head. "No, the opening's too small. You'd have to get right up close to see anything."

"We could climb on those ledges!" Bronte said, her eyes alight with acrobatic zeal. "If we went out the office window, it's just one ledge over and then around the corner to the next ledge. And it's wide! It's way wider than the beam is. I never fall off the beam."

Danny jumped on that quickly, "No, nobody's climbing on any ledges. Ever!"

"What about a fire? If there's a fire, and the stairs are burning, you said we have to go the window for the ladder. So what about then?" Bronte asked, always the stickler for keeping rules straight.

"Okay, okay," Danny sighed, shaking her head slightly, "if there's an emergency, then it's okay to climb on the ledges.

But only for emergencies!"

"Okay," Bronte nodded, settling back to stare with her siblings, at the window and its enigmatic lights, blinking from blue to white, blue to white. "SK?" she asked after another moment of concentration.

"Yeah?" he answered, still staring at the tiny corner of the television screen he could make out through the gap in the blinds.

"Did you open the window too, while you were over there?"

SK shook his head. Of course he didn't open the window. He didn't even realize why Bronte was asking until he heard Danny's shocked intake of breath and Milton's low whistle. Because while the blinds remained resolutely closed, the upper windowpane had been pushed down flush with the lower sash, leaving the window wide open. And it wasn't the only one. Each and every window, all along the front and side of Miss Tonnie's apartment, were wide open to the icy mercies of the frigid night air.

"I hope she didn't turn off the radiators again," Milton murmured.

Certainty and rage pumped through SK's veins. "She didn't turn them off, Milton. The Ghostman did it. Then he blamed it on her." Seeing Milton's skepticism, SK leapt ahead, "don't you see? He can just leave everything and blame her when she—when she—" SK broke off, swallowing his unexpected tears. "We have to help her."

Danny nodded, "When mom and dad get home—"

"No! That's not soon enough!"

"We'll call 911!" Bronte shouted.

"No!" all three of her siblings yelled back before she could even climb off the couch to look for the phone.

"We could use a cell phone. Then they wouldn't have to show up, right? Not like the time when I called from the house phone."

"What would we tell them, Bronte?" Milton asked her. "That our neighbor's windows are open? That there's a weird guy in her apartment who says he's her son, but her son is dead?"

"Yeah?" Bronte offered, hopefully.

"They wouldn't come, and we'd still get in trouble."

"But the weird guy's not there now, see?" Bronte pointed down to the sidewalk, where a pale head seemed to float over a long black coat. The distinctive figure paused briefly, lighting a cigarette, then crossed the street, walking quickly out of sight.

"I'll call Mom now," Danny reassured SK before leaving the room to get her phone.

Milton, Bronte and SK waited, glued to their window, watching that tiny corner of television as though it were the most fascinating show they'd ever seen. Blue, white, blue, white. The colors shifted against the blinds, flickering through the slits and around the edges. Sometime they caught glimpses of a picture through the small opening that SK had managed to make that afternoon, but mostly they just saw the dancing white and black bits on the screen.

"She must have an old TV," Milton commented to himself. "That's snow."

"What's snow?" Bronte asked, looking down at the street and up into the clear skies.

"No, on the TV, all those little black and white bits moving around, that's called snow. It's visual static," he added, for no one's benefit, but his own.

"That's snow. It's snowing," SK whispered, staring at that glowing corner with renewed intensity. "And it's doing the same thing it did the first night that Danny and I saw the Ghostman. The changing colors, that's from switching channels, see?" He tapped the glass in rhythm with the changes. Color, static, color, static, color, static. Then slower—color beat, static beat. Three times. The pattern kept repeating. Three fast switches, three slow switches. "The snow," SK breathed with dawning recognition, "is a signal! It's in code!"

"What?" Milton asked.

"It's Morse code! It's SOS, in Morse code!" SK was off the couch now. He twitched and paced through the room, too caught up in the gravity of his realization to stay still.

"Mom left her phone here, and Dad's not answering. He probably forgot to charge it again." Danny said, pausing in the doorway, as she saw SK's frenetic pacing. "Are you okay?"

"No! I am not okay! SOS means it's an emergency! We have to call the police, right now!" SK erupted, finally able to focus his fears into words. Tortured images writhed through his brain. He was torn between wanting to rush to somewhere to find help and staying right where he was, to keep that flickering signal locked in his sight.

"SK," Milton said seriously, "we still really don't have a reason to call the police. But," he added quickly to cut off his brother's protests, "I think you're right. We have to do something. Danny, you keep trying Dad's phone. I'll run to campus and try to find them at that reception."

"That will take too long!" SK agonized, remembering the horror and helplessness he'd seen in Miss Tonnie's eyes that afternoon.

"They're at the faculty club, and that's on this side of the Midway," Milton told them, already pulling his sweater on.

"Milton, you can't go there on your own, it's dark and —"Danny stopped talking, looking puzzled. SK was so caught up in his own worrying that it took him a moment to notice her silence. Danny's forehead wrinkled with concern and she stood there, looking around for a moment before asking, "Where's Bronte?"

Milton groaned, but immediately knelt to check behind the couch and under the console table, while Danny headed for the closet. It was SK who spotted her first though, because he just couldn't tear himself away from the window. "There she is!" he called to his brother and sister, pointing through the window at a small, determined, black-haired girl standing on Dad's office desk, carefully raising the top window sash.

"Dammit!" Danny swore, already on her way down the hall, Milton at her heels. SK followed them to the office, too antsy and nervous to stay still, and watched while they bustled Bronte off the desk and out of the room. Listening to his siblings argue in the hallway, his attention was drawn inexorably to the still-open window, separated by a mere six feet from Miss Tonnie's, also-open window.

The screen came off easily, sliding into the room with only two puffs of dust, writhing like thin streams of smoke from each side. SK slipped out onto the ledge. His mind made up, SK didn't pause to think about the distance down or the cold air on his head, neck, ankles and arms. He didn't let the bite of the rough stone on his palms and his knees distract him from his goal. He had to help Miss Tonnie. She was his responsibility.

Rounding the corner was easier once he stood up, so he could just step over the gap, rather than bending his whole body if he were still crawling. Once around the corner he stayed upright, since it was Miss Tonnie's upper sash that was open. It would be much easier, he thought, to step in, rather than having to lift himself up from a crouch.

Gripping the top of the sash with one hand, SK struggled with the screen for several seconds. His fingers were on the wrong side of it to get any purchase and they were so numb from the cold that he couldn't tell the difference between screen, sash, stone or glass. SK tried to study the screen and window, but his face was beginning to ache. Tears of frustration stung his eyes and his whole body shook with cold. Leaning his forehead on the glass, SK made the mistake of opening his eyes and looking down for the first time.

SK had spent way too much time playing with this super-bouncy power ball gravity tester not to know that three floors was a long, long way and that he was neither super nor bouncy. Swallowing his fears, SK closed his eyes briefly and pulled his arm back for one powerful push, popping the screen out of the window and into the room. Breathing hard now — whether from exertion or fear he didn't know — SK swung his leg up and over into the room. His toes were still several inches above the sill, so for one dizzying second SK straddled the inch wide window sash, feet dangling in the air on either side, before ducking his head and rolling into the room. He hung for the briefest of moments, entangled in the slats and cords of the blinds before his weight tore them away from their mountings and he fell to the floor in a clatter of metal, plastic and boy.

"Miss Tonnie," he called out, even as he struggled free of the cords and bent screen frame. "Miss Tonnie, I got your message. Are you—" the words froze in SK's throat. By the light of the silently flickering TV, he could see that Miss Tonnie lay just as he'd left her earlier that day, only the blanket had been removed and tossed across the room. She was also, SK realized with growing horror, soaking wet. Two empty glasses lay on the floor next to her, but there was no way they had held enough liquid to make her as wet as she was. There was also a pitcher of water, half full, stuck haphazardly among the books under the TV. From head to foot, Miss Tonnie was sopping. Her left hand, gripping the TV remote with rigid fingers, waved erratically in his direction, her head rolling toward him, but unable to turn.

"It's okay, Miss Tonnie, it's going to be okay," he found himself telling her as he scooped up the blanket and moved to her side. "That was real cool, the TV Morse code," SK continued. She was shaking quite badly he realized, her body wracked and contorted by the cold. Not knowing what else to do, he tucked the blanket against her. Her nightgown twisted grotesquely around her limbs in stiff, frozen folds which cracked under his hands. The windows had been open for a long time, he guessed. And the radiators, he was certain, had been turned off for even longer. How long does it take to freeze wet cloth, he wondered. He had never done temperature experiments. But SK knew, even without the help of scientific data, that Miss Tonnie was too cold. She was much too cold.

He ran to the windows, one by one, pushing the sashes up and twisting the locks to hold them closed. The noise of the sashes slamming home in their frames masked the pounding at first. At the third window, though, he realized that someone was at the front door, knocking. His heart jumped in his chest, slamming into his throat.

"SK," he heard, muffled but clear, "SK, it's me, Danny. SK! Are you in there? SK?" With Danny's help he might be able to get Miss Tonnie off that wet couch and figure how to turn on the radiators, he thought, already running to the door.

Throwing the bolts, he dragged his sister through the door and down the hallway.

"What about the door?" Danny asked, stumbling after him.

"She's in here, we need to move her and get her warm," he told her breathlessly. "Leave the door open, it's warmer in the stairwell."

Danny's eyes widened and she sucked in her breath as they came into the living room.

"Gees, it's a freezer in here. Oh! SK, is she, is she—" Danny's words trailed off, but her body leapt into action. With her phone in one hand, Danny ran to the radiator, twisting the valve open. The radiator hissed to life, while Danny hissed with frustration. "Dad's still not answering, but Milton took Bronte with him to get Mom and Dad. It's only like fifteen minutes to campus, like five to find them, fifteen back, so—"

And then Danny said a word that SK had never heard her say before and she got very, very pale. Way paler than her normal pale, which was saying something. SK had thought he'd felt cold before, but the ice that crept up his spine while he stood there with his back to the hallway and the open door turned him cold from the inside out. He didn't want to turn around, but he forced himself to do it. He knew what he'd see. But knowing didn't make it any less scary.

Ghostman stood in the hall, framed by the light from the stairwell behind him. Light from the silent television lit the hallway just enough to flicker reflections in the picture frames' glass and in Ghostman's yellow eyes. He stepped into the apartment and pulled the door closed behind him. Then he smiled.

"Well aren't you two just the best little neighbors? But I don't need your help. Not a bit." The smile never left his face as he strolled down the hall. "You should probably get along home, now, don't you think?" He stopped in front of SK, tilting his head slightly to scrutinize the ruins beneath the window. "Now, that's not good, is it?"

SK opened his mouth to answer, but nothing came out. He tried to shake his head, but that didn't work either. He couldn't see what Danny was doing, but she wasn't saying anything either. The only sounds in the room were Miss Tonnie's rasping breath and the wet wheezing of the radiator. Ghostman pulled a cigarette from his pocket, contemplating it for a moment, then lit it before speaking.

"You went and closed all the windows. And got that radiator back on, now didn't you?"

Still unable to speak, SK found himself backing up toward Danny as Ghostman gradually advanced toward him. "Now what am I going to do?" Ghostman asked, gliding even closer. "Well, I thought ice would be great. It's slow, but it does the trick, you know, at least for a crazy old lady. But you two, you're too quick for ice, aren't you? So I'm thinking that maybe fire might do me a favor. What do you think? Oh, I'm so sorry, no smoking in the house," Ghostman's smile widened and he leaned over, carefully smothering his cigarette in the flesh of Miss Tonnie's right arm.

She still couldn't make words, but her sounds, well, SK had no doubt what they meant. Flinging the full force of his big-for-his-age, husky-wearing, oughta-play-pee-wee-football body at Ghostman's arm, SK latched on. Then he bit him. Hard. The good part was that the cigarette thing stopped, and that was really all SK cared about. The bad part was that Ghostman didn't need a cigarette to hurt people.

"You fucking little shit!" Ghostman snarled, flinging

SK off of his arm and onto the floor.

"Stop hurting her! Stop!" SK managed to gasp out just before Ghostman kicked him in the back of the head. He was too stunned to move, so he took the full force of the next blow, which sent him flying into coffee table. Remotes, books, dishes, table and SK all skittered along the floor, banging into the bookcase and then landing against the wall on the far side of the living room. SK heard his sister scream as he twisted through the room, and then things went dark.

※　　※　　※

"SHUT UP, BITCH," Ghostman's voice cut through the blackness into SK's skull, "or I'll cut this little cocksucker." Danny's screaming choked off, swallowed by sobs. It must have only been a few seconds that he'd been out, SK thought, as he became aware again. He could hear Danny crying and Miss Tonnie's wordless protests. He could feel hands on his head and neck, holding him near the floor. Not wanting to make it real, SK resigned himself to opening his eyes anyway.

The first thing he saw was Danny's cell phone. Well, half of Danny's cell phone. It had been snapped in half, the screen cracked and plastic crushed. It was difficult to see with his head twisted toward the floor. The fingers of Ghostman's right hand, SK noticed now that they were so close to his face, were stained the same grimy yellow as his teeth, and they held a slender, sliver blade which gently traced the line of SK's jaw. Ghostman's left hand pressed against SK's mouth and nose

173

making it hard to breath, each finger bruising and cold. Very cold. A small part of SK wondered how a person could have such cold hands and still be walking around. Maybe Ghostman was who he said he was. Maybe his hand was so cold because he was dead. The bigger part of SK's mind knew that wasn't true, though. The bigger part of his brain told SK to keep still, told him to act small and dumb and quiet. So that's what SK did. Even though he could feel blood running down the back of his head.

"Just hold out your hands like a good little girl," Ghostman said, letting SK's head drop to the floor. SK hadn't thought it would hurt so much, since the floor seemed so close, but he was wrong. The pain had colors, mostly red and black, and it was all he could do not throw up. The only bright side was that SK had landed with his head facing Danny where she hunched against the wall. She looked scared, but okay. For now.

Ghostman began tying Danny up using the cords from the blinds. "Too bad we don't have time to play, but we've got a deadline now, don't we? I'd let the old lady tell you all about my games, but she can't tell nobody nothing, can she?" Done tying, Ghostman hadn't even bothered to cut the strings from the blinds, instead using the slats to bind Danny to the radiator. He smiled at his handiwork, stroking the edge of Danny's collar with his knife.

The nausea came back, all of a sudden, much stronger than the first time. SK groaned, shifting on the floor. "Shhh," a voice whispered, tickling his ear with warm air. There was no one behind him, he knew. No one to whisper in his ear. Miss Tonnie, Danny and Ghostman were all on the other side of the room. SK wasn't sure what was harder, not throwing up from pain when he turned his head to the other side, or finding the courage to look for someone who couldn't be there. Somehow, he did both.

In the corner, crouched down on one knee and staring directly at SK, was Walter Booker Huguley. The late Walter Booker Huguley. He was dressed in his full uniform and he looked just like the picture on the wall—just like the photo in the paper. His obituary photo. He looked pretty good for a dead guy, SK thought woozily. Walter held one finger up to his lips. Then he lowered his finger to point at the gap between the upended table and the wall, inches away from SK's right hand. SK squinted into the space, trying to process the two objects he saw. One he recognized easily. It was his super-bouncy power-ball gravity-tester. The other, he thought, was the TV remote control. But no, he realized suddenly, Miss Tonnie was still holding the remote. The grey plastic rectangle on the floor —that was a phone. It was Miss Tonnie's phone. And not a cell phone, either. It was her house phone.

He reached out, pulling the phone close to dial, then stopped in fear. Ghostman was humming, doing something behind him, but SK couldn't be sure that he wouldn't hear the beep of the phone buttons. He glanced up at Walter, who smiled at him, nodding. So SK pressed the on button and then, quickly muffling the dial tone with his palm over the earpiece, he pressed three more. The angle of his body, he trusted, kept the phone from view. His palm, he hoped, would keep it quiet. But dialing 911 wouldn't do any good if he couldn't get his message across. Walter was still in the corner, urging him on silently. So SK took a deep breath, and called out.

"Untie my sister and let us go." His voice was weaker than he'd hoped, but he was pretty sure it was loud enough for the person on the other end of the phone. With his hand over the earpiece, he couldn't hear them, but he could feel vibrations against his palm, so he felt confident that they were talking to him. Seeing Walter? That gave him confidence too, for some reason. "Stop hurting Miss Tonnie, let us go," he said lifting his head, which hurt, but he had to. He needed to see where Ghostman was so he could keep the phone out of sight.

"What did you say, little man?" Ghostman asked, turning to face SK.

"Why won't you let us go? Why do you keep hurting our neighbor, Mrs. Huguley?" It was hard for SK to keep talking, but he knew he had to. He really just wanted to sleep, but he knew he had to make sure that the people at 911 knew that he needed help. "Why," he asked, his voice faint, but steady, "why would you say she's your mother when she's not? Why did you burn her like that?"

"Why, why, why," Ghostman whined back at him, mocking. "Because I want to and I can." He strode over to pick up a bowl from the detritus on the floor near SK. Crouching down next to SK, Ghostman looked him right in the eye. SK stared right back at him. Every nerve in SK's body was on fire. All he could think about was the phone under his hand, and what would happen if Ghostman saw it. "Maybe she likes it," Ghostman whispered, "maybe she asked me to do it."

Still staring at SK, Ghostman's face split into a grin, and picking up one of the paperbacks from the floor, he sliced out a handful of pages, crumpling them into the bowl. Then he walked over to the television, placed the bowl on the top shelf of the bookcase, leaning back a little to reach under the bulk of the TV, which loomed over him and was still the only source of light in the room. Ghostman pulled out another cigarette and some matches, leaning one shoulder against the heavy frame of Miss Tonnie's outdated Sony. After lighting his cigarette and taking a deep drag, he folded the cover of the matchbook back, bent the matches into a fan shape and settled them on top of the wads of paper. He looked at it for a moment before grabbing another book off the shelf to sacrifice as well.

"She's not your mother," SK said, trying to remember why he was supposed to be talking. There was something important he was supposed to tell someone, right? Why couldn't he remember, he wondered.

"She is not my mother, little man is correct! Two points," Ghostman flipped his hands over his head, tossing one of the crumpled pages at SK's head.

The page landed on the floor next to his face and SK stared, mesmerized as the paper turned red, soaking up the blood from where it pooled beneath him. A boot, black and shiny, pushed the paper aside, and SK felt warm fingers brush across his forehead. He couldn't hear anything, but somehow he knew that Walter needed him to stay awake, needed him to keep talking. "She's not your mother, and you can't be here!" SK managed to say.

"She's not my mother, but I can too be here," Ghostman taunted. "In fact, I get paid to be here. What could be better than that? I know! I get paid to be here and to do what I want and to take what I want and she can't do a goddamn motherfucking thing about it. Mother fucking," he laughed. "Now that's funny, 'cause she's not my momma."

SK didn't think it was funny. SK thought it was sick and scary and he hoped that whoever was on the other side of the phone call thought it was sick and scary too, so they would send some police cars. "You took her money. You took her a hundreds thousands dollars, didn't you?" SK wasn't sure if that was how you said it, but he thought it was close enough that the people on the phone would know what he meant.

"Damn straight I did. What's a twisted, broken old lady need with all that money? She didn't do nothing for it. Did she get shot at? Did she have Taliban on her ass everyday? I don't think so," Ghostman shook his head.

"Did you?" SK asked.

"Fuck no. I ain't dumb enough to sign up for that shit. You dumb enough to sign up to get shot at, you deserve getting shot." Ghostman eyed his paper monument, "Maybe I should put this in the kitchen. It'll take too long for the gas to get in here. And we've only got what," he glanced at his watch, "another twenty minutes before your family gets here. Bet you'd love it if they got here in time for the party. It's going to be hot, hot, hot!" Ghostman laughed at his joke, while gathering his paper pile.

His chuckling cut short as a black plastic rectangle hit him in the back of the head. "Shit!" he whipped around searching for the source. Miss Tonnie waved her empty left hand at him. There was no mistaking the expression on the left side of her face for anything other than triumph. "Bitch, that ain't going to keep you from burning. You and these kids. They're on you, bitch. They on you," he finished, advancing toward her. He stopped, almost immediately, puzzled by a rhythmic thumping behind him. He turned and saw, well, SK wasn't sure what Ghostman saw. What SK saw was his super-bouncy-power ball gravity tester bouncing up and down, up and down; thrown and caught by Walter Booker Huguley. In the background, far up the street, SK heard the distant voice of a police car siren. In time with each other, as though choreographed, the ball and the siren rose and fell together.

Ghostman stared, his eyes and head tracking the ball in its arcs, up and down, up and down, as the siren's wail grew closer. Walter's face was deceptively calm but SK could feel the waves of anger rolling off of him, growing with each bounce. Walter let the ball drop, one final time, and though it continued to bounce, each repetition lost a little height, a little speed, until the ball dribbled to the fbor, rolling past Ghostman's feet and into the bookcase where the TV perched. The siren, likewise, rose for one final note in its aria before falling silent, very, very close by.

"What the fuck," Ghostman muttered, leaning over slowly to pick up the small rubber orb from where it lay in a puddle of water. As he did so, his shoulder bumped the bookcase, ever so slightly. Far, far too slightly to explain what happened next. Since the police weren't there to see it, their report just listed it as an accident. But SK knew better.

SK knew because he watched as Chief Master Sergeant Walter Booker Huguley pushed Miss Tonnie's ancient, huge, and oh-so-very heavy television off of the bookcase and onto the head of the man who stooped beneath it.

The TV, still on, landed in a crash of glass and a fiery storm of electricity directly on his head. Sparks crisscrossed Ghostman's skin, burning so bright that they lit the inside of SK's eyelids for hours—days even—afterward. The ball rolled gently back into the fingers of SK's right hand.

The last thing SK saw in Miss Tonnie's living room that night before finally losing consciousness was Walter Booker Huguley, gently stroking his mother's hand before quietly melting away into memory.

THE AFTERNOON OF THE STORM

by

Kirk VanDyke

THE BAR AT the base of the snow-capped mountain was empty except for a few regulars smoking Camels and watching reruns of Bonanza. A pair of men sat together at the corner of the bar. They didn't say much, but occasionally one of them would tell a joke and both would give a half-hearted laugh, as if they'd told each other the same jokes a hundred times. The remaining patrons were retired and scraggly. They hadn't seen a razor among them in years. One might even think they hadn't seen a bar of soap in a few days either. Except for the TV, the bar was quiet. There was a thin cloud of smoke overhead. No one seemed to mind.

Bill sat in the middle and looked at the beers on tap. He wanted one, but knew he shouldn't, since the sheriff was on his way. The bartender, Ethan, looked over. Ethan was a middle aged man from the south who had escaped to the mountains from a corporate job. He still looked professional, though. His flannel shirt couldn't hide his button-down past.

"Hey, Bill, what you having today?" Ethan smiled like the salesman he once had been. He'd never lost that Atlanta feel. Maybe it was something to do with the accent.

"I want a beer but I better have some coffee, if you've got a pot made." Bill shifted in his seat and removed his ball cap. It was dirty, like the rest of him, and faded from the sun.

Ethan brought Bill some coffee and a few sugar

packets. He said, "Did you ever hear back about that dead guy you found near your place last winter?"

Bill took off his cap and placed it on the bar. He scratched his curly hair and then picked up his cup of coffee. He didn't want the sugar. Ethan should have known that by now. He took a sip and a little ran down his graying beard. He said, "It's still unsolved, but I found his partner this morning in a thawed-out snowdrift about a mile from where I found the other guy. The sheriff and search and rescue are on their way. That's why I'm not having a beer today, even though I need one. I need to stay sober for the police."

Larry, one of the regulars, had seemed engrossed in the television. But he suddenly turned around. He was still wearing his Carhart jacket despite the wood stove near the pool table. The stove was burning even though it was 40 degrees outside. "Bill, you found the other one?"

The other patrons looked at Bill.

"Yeah, this morning. He's partially buried still but it looks to me like he got stuck in some of that blowdown up there. Got hung up or something."

"That was a hell of a storm," someone said.

Another added, "They was fools to be out in that weather."

Everyone nodded in agreement. It was the worst storm of the year, probably three or four inches of snow per hour complete with 60 mph winds. It drifted like hell and set up hard. Plus, with the beetle kill in the area, dead trees blew over and made a real tangle of the forest. It was pure hell moving through that area now. A person had to crawl over so many fallen trees that it made travel real slow.

The door opened. Jacob, in his brown sheriff's outfit, looked out of place amid the beer signs. He walked straight toward Bill. Bill thought Jacob was a bit out of shape to be crawling over that forest, but he was the man on the scene the first time, when they had trudged up there with snow shoes. Jacob had seemed like he was going to have a heart attack before they got there, but he'd persevered.

Behind Jacob were Rob and Steve, the search and rescue guys. They were young and fit and could haul a wood stove out of the middle of the forest if they needed to. Rob, the slightly larger one, said hi to Bill. Then Steve put out his hand. It was clean, as if he had an office job.

Bill shook it and said, "Well, let's get this over with."

Ethan said, "Coffee's on the house, Bill. Come back later and I'll buy you a beer.

❊   ❊   ❊

THE DRIVE UP the mountain to the lodge was about seven miles but it seemed like twelve. It was slow and winding and most of the good views were obscured by lodgepole pines lining the highway. Bill drove in front in his old white GMC pickup truck. Most of the paint had peeled off, and there were signs of rust creeping through in spots, but the engine and the 4WD worked fine, so that was good enough for Bill. Behind him were two official vehicles—one a sheriff's SUV and the other a

Ford F-250 with a topper over the bed. They were new and clean and quiet. Bill's truck had straight pipes and roared up the hills in a perfectly timed rhythm.

He passed several trailheads and drove farther. Two campgrounds, both closed, were to his left beside a small stream running high with snow melt. As they ventured higher, snow began to appear in drifts in the trees. Water was running off the mountain out of these drifts in countless intermittent streams, making the entire area seem damp. Above the second campground and beyond a small meadow, Bill pulled into the sagging log lodge where he was the caretaker. The other two trucks followed.

The lodge was an old research camp built by the CCC. It was made of large lodgepole pine trunks with vaulted ceilings and an old spruce trunk still in the middle of the building. In fact, for some reason unknown to Bill, they had built the structure around this massive spruce. It came up through the floor and went straight up to the ceiling, where it was cut off. Above it, in the middle of a large room, the roof had begun to sag. The place needed work. Everyone knew that. But who was going to do it? It was a slice of history in the mountains, now in disuse, and was soon to be condemned by the Forest Service if major repairs weren't undertaken. Bill knew the current owners wouldn't sink a dime into the place. He was only up there to keep vandals out. $550 a month. Just watch over the place. That was his job.

The sheriff got out of his SUV and said, "So how far up is he?"

Rob and Steve were already standing near Bill. Steve said, "Is he up by the lake?"

"No," Bill said. "He's down near the creek. He almost made it out. He had the direction despite the storm. Guy knew what he was doing?"

"If he knew what he was doing," said the sheriff, "he'd still be alive."

"Well, it was a hell of a storm," said Rob. He went to the back of his truck and opened the topper. "Steve, you ready to haul this thing?" He slid a sled with handles on the ends out of the back.

"Let's get this over with." Said Steve.

"That seems to be the consensus," said Bill. He started walking down a dirt road. "He's up here."

Bill walked in front of Steve and Rob, each holding an end of the sled, and behind them lumbered Jacob. They walked past a few small cabins with the windows broken and roofs collapsing, past a large spruce tree and into the snow. The melting drifts were four feet deep in places and the bare spots were simply pools of water on top of needles. They crossed Sally Creek—not large but definitely high during the snow melt. Then they wandered up a faint trail through spruce and fr, post-holing in the deep drifts and making slow progress. Jacob began to fall back.

"Let's wait for the sheriff," said Rob. And he sat his end of the sled down on a drift.

Jacob came along in a few minutes. He was out of breath. After a few more minutes, he said, "Damn, this was a bitch in the winter but it's worse now."

Bill pulled a can of Copenhagen out of his shirt pocket and took a pinch. He spat on the dirty snow. "We'll cut up the hill here and then he's a few hundred yards back. Like I said before, he almost made it out alive." He started to walk up the hill, post-holing in the deep snow.

No one said a word. As they got to the top of the hill and it started to level out, the blowdown was really bad. They had to crawl over downfall and under snags, sinking to their thighs in the melting snow. Some of the snow was so compacted that they stayed on top and the walking was easy, but then they would suddenly break through. It jarred their backs. Progress was slow. Jacob fell farther behind but the rest pushed on without him. He could follow their trail. They were plowing a big swath through the forest.

"Son of a bitch," said Rob when he saw the half-buried body. There was a cluster of fallen tree trunks near the legs.

"Serves him right."

"What do you mean?" said Bill. He spit a wad of tobacco juice on the snow.

"Guy poisons his friend and then dies trying to escape."

"Cyanide is what the tox report said." Steve sat down on a fallen log.

"I don't know," said Bill. "Sounds a bit fishy if you ask me."

Jacob still hadn't arrived, but they could hear him cussing behind them. The temperature was falling some and the wind picked up. Everyone was sweating and standing around made them feel cold, like it was winter again. Jacob fell in behind them and fished a cigarette out of his coat pocket. He lit it, took a drag, and coughed. "Let me see this," he said. He coughed again and breathed heavily. "Can we move some of this snow off him?"

Steve and Rob started to remove some of the snow with a small shovel they'd brought. They exposed his thighs and some of the area around his snow shoes. The snow shoes were lodged between fallen trees. Steve said, "Looks like he got stuck here and then froze to death trying to get out. Zero degrees and 60 mph winds. He didn't have a chance."

"Don't move him," said Jacob. "I need to get a good look at this." He pulled out a camera and took a few pictures. Then he stood deep in thought for a few minutes. "Looks like we got our killer." He said.

"What do you mean?" said Bill. "The other guy was just sitting near his tent, near his camp stove, buried in snow. He had a tea cup in his lap. There was nothing about a struggle or anything like that."

"Cyanide," said Jacob. "They found cyanide in his system and our dead friend here, John Roberts, worked in a soils lab. Had cyanide at his disposal."

"But I hear they were friends," said Bill.

"Some friends," said Steve.

"How did you manage to find these two guys?" asked Rob. He turned away and looked at a Steller's Jay. It lit on a tree above them.

"It's my back yard," Bill said. "The first time I heard

someone was missing, out near Swastika Lake, I went out to see if I could find them. Sure enough, I found the camp. It was half buried in snow, but the yellow tent really stood out. I first saw the tent and I thought, great, I've found them. Big mistake. Got up to the tent and I see a guy all purple, slumped in a seated position. What was his name?"

"Scott Thorn," said Jacob.

"Well, I found Scott Thorn too late," said Bill. He shifted in the snow. "Then, I knew with the thaw that I'd find this other fellow because he never showed up, either. Just figured he had to be nearby since no one ever heard from him again." He took off his ball cap and scratched his head.

❀   ❀   ❀

THE BAR ALWAYS held the same afternoon crowd and each person had his stool, day after day. They never really ventured into the mountains. They simply walked to the bar around noon each day, drank until dinner time, and walked home when the bar began to fill with the evening crowd. Larry sat near the TV, chain smoking Camels. Jim and Tom sat together, seldom speaking. Bill took his spot between them and ordered a Bud from Ethan. Ethan was in a particularly good mood. He said he liked summer in the mountains more than any other season. And he took advantage of the nice weather. Before work, he went on an extended hike with his dog. Alone, of course.

Bill looked at the TV and sipped his Bud. He'd seen this Bonanza episode several times. No telling how many times Larry had watched it. The door opened and in walked a middle-aged woman, short, with hiking apparel that looked newly purchased. She wore a hint of makeup and stood by the pool table looking perplexed. It seemed she had never been in such a place before. She walked to the bar and Ethan smiled at her. Bill knew who it was but he didn't say anything. He turned his back to her and took a long drink of beer.

"What can I get you?" asked Ethan. He smiled.

"Nothing, thanks. I'm looking for Bill Thompson. Is he here?"

"He's sitting next to you."

Bill turned with a beer in his hand. "You must be Alison," he said. "Nice to meet you." He didn't shake her hand.

She smiled and sat down next to him. "You're a hard man to get a hold of. But thank you for meeting me," she said.

He sat his beer down on the bar. There was only a quarter left in it. He ordered another from Ethan. He said, "I don't get cell reception up at the lodge and there's no land line up there. Sorry I couldn't meet with you this winter when you came out. And, by the way, sorry for your loss."

Alison pulled out some cash. She said, "Thank you. I'll get his beer."

"Both of them?" asked Ethan.

"Yes." She turned back to Bill. "I was hoping you'd have time to show me where my brother died this winter. I don't know, it's hard because he was the only family I had left.

Now it's just me. I'm trying to piece this together and bring some closure to it. At least for me. I know we'll never know what truly happened up there."

Larry turned around and exhaled smoke. He snubbed out his butt and fished another cigarette out of the pack. "That was a hell of a storm they got trapped in. Worst one of the year, maybe the last few years."

Alison turned and said, "Yes, that's what I've heard, but my brother, Scott, had survived bad storms in the past. For that matter, so had his friend."

"Damned shame," Tom interrupted, and then smiled uncomfortably, as if he felt awkward about butting in.

She turned back to Bill. "I don't know if I believe what the sheriff says about the event. They were best friends."

Bill finished his first beer and pushed the glass back on the bar. Then he moved his full glass closer to him and sipped from it. He felt nervous meeting her but he didn't know why. The dead guys were all anyone cared to talk about when he was around. He wanted to be done with it but he felt an obligation to this woman, this stranger. He looked at her. She looked like she'd come from a city back east. She seemed entirely out of place in the bar, in the mountains, in anything but a nice car stuck in traffic.

"I'll take you up there when I'm done with this beer. And by the way, thanks. You didn't have to do that." Bill said. He smiled.

"It's the least I can do. Is it far? Do I need to bring anything special?" Alison shifted in her seat. Her legs didn't touch the floor and it made her look like a child in the presence of these men. Bill followed her eyes as she glanced around the bar. A few elk and deer heads hung on the walls. A bear hide was spread out on the far one, with its claws still attached.

"Maybe a bottle of water. And a jacket in case we get an afternoon thunderstorm. They don't tend to last long but they can be intense at times."

"I've got both those things in a backpack. I checked the weather and it said clear today." She said.

"That's for town," said Ethan. "We get more weather up here. Are you sure you don't want anything? A Coke?"

"A Coke will be fine, thanks." She said. She wrinkled her nose at the cigarette smoke drifting across the bar.

"So what have you been doing with yourself in town?" Bill said.

"Mostly going through my brother's things, what's left of them. He didn't have much. He was a real minimalist. I put his stuff in storage this winter so this time I'm clearing it out. I'm giving it to friends. And I've been reading his journal, which has been hard."

"I bet," said Bill. He took a long drink of beer. "Find anything interesting in it?"

"Well, yes, in fact." She said. She pulled the Coke closer but didn't take a sip. "My brother was schizophrenic. He'd been taking his meds for years and done really well on them. No major hallucinations or episodes. I don't know if you know anything about schizophrenia, but it can be a real nightmare. And, after doing so well for all these years, he

194

decided to go off them."

"He was some kind of researcher, wasn't he?" That's what Bill had heard.

"Yes, he was looking into plant uptake of precious metals. I don't know, he thought it had some exploratory potential or something. Anyway, everything was going well and then he decided to go off the meds and he started hearing things again." She sipped her Coke. She seemed nervous talking about this to a stranger, but, perhaps because Bill was the guy who found her brother, she continued. "I don't know if you know anything about schizophrenia or not, Bill, but my brother had begun to hear voices again and see things that couldn't have been there. Most of the journaling was about research before he went off his meds, but then it changed. I found a poem in there, written a week before his death, and it seems to be a suicide poem."

"No shit," said Bill. "You think your brother killed himself up there?"

"I do. And I think his friend freaked out and went to get help but didn't make it."

"I wondered about that myself," said Bill. He pulled out his can of Copenhagen and took a pinch. Then he drained his beer. "Thanks, Ethan." He turned to Alison. "Let's finish this conversation up by the lake."

❊   ❊   ❊

Bill didn't park at the lodge; he parked at a trailhead down the hill. He got out of his truck and walked over to Alison's compact rental car. She paused, perhaps wondering what she was doing, following this grizzly backwoods man into the woods alone. She'd probably never do such a thing at home. Perhaps she didn't feel she had a choice. Maybe she felt compelled to see where her brother had died, in a blizzard, with only his best friend at his side. Bill watched her get out of the car and open the back door to pull out her backpack. Bill had nothing but a thick flannel shirt, unbuttoned, over a T-shirt. His jeans were dirty with grease.

"I decided to park here," said Bill, "because there's a trail that loops around the back side of the lake. It's a little longer but we don't have to cross as much blowdown this way, so it's shorter in the long run."

"Is this where you found Scott's friend?" She asked.

"No, he was in the blowdown closer to the lodge." Bill began to walk down a small dirt trail. It smelled of pines and was dry. All the snow was gone for the year, but he knew it could start again anytime. He'd seen snow on July 4th before. It didn't accumulate, but it fell out of the sky in large, tumbling flakes.

Alison followed, walking a few feet behind him. "How long have you lived up here?"

"About four years." And he left it at that. He took another pinch of Copenhagen.

They walked uphill at a brisk pace, Alison struggling to keep up. She looked around nervously, as if wondering where in the hell she was. Or perhaps wondering whether she could get back on her own. It was simple enough—just follow the trail back the way they had come. She looked uncomfortable: she was out of shape for this.

Bill turned off the trail. He stopped and waited for her. "The lake's back here a quarter mile. We'll just have to wind through the trees and follow the slight ridgeline up ahead. You OK?"

"Yes, thank you," she said. "Do you think this is the way my brother came?"

"Most likely." He began to walk again, meandering between fallen trees, ducking under overhanging branches, and making methodical progress up a slight rise.

Alison began to fall behind. She had trouble getting over a fallen cluster of trees. Bill waited for her on the other side. "It's not much farther," he said. And then he began to walk again. They began to climb a crest and, then, through the trees, they could see a large lake. It was deep blue and placid. Bill descended the ridgeline and followed the contour of the lake about a hundred feet above it. Alison followed as best she could. She had a hard time keeping up with his pace.

Suddenly, at the lake's edge, near a small opening, Bill stopped. "Well, this is it," he said. He pointed to a little stream coming out of the lake's end. "I found your brother down there. He was sitting outside his tent. And his tent was open. Snow had drifted inside. We found both of their gear inside, including a GPS unit. That's what makes me think your brother's friend, John Roberts, freaked out and tried to get some help. He just left in a hurry and headed directly for my lodge. It's that direction." He said and he pointed to the southeast. "Do you want to go down there?"

"Yes, please." She said, and she followed him down the hill until they stopped in a small opening.

"You okay?" He said.

"I'm just thinking this is so beautiful. My brother must have chosen it for a reason."

"Well, it's pretty isolated for one. No one comes back here, especially in the winter. There's too much blowdown as you've probably noticed."

Alison sat down on a rock. She looked around but didn't say anything for a while. A bald eagle flew over the lake and lit on a tall fir tree near the edge. She reached in her backpack and pulled out a bottle of water. She took a drink. Then she pulled out a small digital camera and stood up. "Do you mind if I take your picture?" She said.

"No," he said. "Feel free."

She took a few pictures, one of Bill and several of the lake, making sure to get the camp site in each of them. She began to cry. She said, "My brother went from being a straight-A student to failing out of school when he was twenty. He assaulted a campus cop, but they didn't press charges as long as he'd receive psychiatric help. That's the first time he was hospitalized. He got out but didn't stay on his meds. He went through countless jobs until an old girlfriend told him she'd like to get back together with him on the condition that he stay on antipsychotics. And he did. He did great. He went back to school, got straight A's again, held a job. He stayed with her. I just don't understand why he went off them again." She wiped her face.

Bill said, "You'll probably never know. Did he still have the same girlfriend?"

"No, they broke up. She wanted kids and he didn't. He didn't want to get married."

Bill broke off a stalk of grass and sucked on it. He said, "When I was in college I had a friend who was schizophrenic. He was brilliant but all he could do was wash dishes part time at this small restaurant near campus. But he was still a voracious reader. He read everything. I lost touch with him after I finished. I've often wondered what he's up to, but we were both hermits. There was no way to keep in touch."

Alison stopped crying. She said, "What did you study in college?"

"History," he said. "I even stuck around and did a master's. Not that I ever did anything with my degree."

"You sound like my brother. I don't know that he had any career plans, either. He just liked being around a university. I guess he felt accepted there."

Alison reached in a pack and pulled out a box. "There's one more thing I want to do here before I leave."

Bill knew what she was doing. He said, "I didn't know your brother, but I think he would have liked your being here. And bringing him back."

Club

Pandimonium

by

Christalea McMullin

THE WINTER MOON glistened on the snow. Though Lena's breath crystallized at her lips, she felt warm under her black velvet cloak. Her feet crunched on the snow-covered path that led her to the heart of Club Pandemonium's garden. The garden, mostly unused this time of year, had one solitary set of footprints. She followed these quietly, though her mind raced on, blistering with annoyance.

Lena believed the footprints to be Derrick's. The size matched his, as did the slight cleft in the print. Lena felt her irritation grow. She had been at the after party of her best friend's rendition of *King Henry the Eighth*. Lena loved opera, she loved her friend, and if she had left the party early because of some stupid joke, Derrick was in for a bloody lip. Figuratively. She had too much class to hit him with her fist.

The clear night was thick with silence. The only sound Lena heard was the startlingly loud crunch of her own footsteps. That bothered her. Where were the owls? Where was the rustling of night animals? Nervously, she pulled out her cell phone. Her fingers trembled as she flicked to his last message. The glow of her phone spoiled her night vision. She stumbled to the stone bench where they were to meet. She pushed the snow off and settled down to wait.

"If it was such an emergency, why am I waiting for you, Derrick?" She muttered to herself. "And why in the blazes are we meeting outside in the middle of winter?"

Lena's phone chirped that it was now four in the morning. At that moment, her whole world shifted. A cloud—the only one in the sky, and one Lena was certain hadn't been there a minute ago—was passing over the moon.

Derrick's shout rang out like the crack of a gun. Derrick sprinted away from the old oak at the top of the hill. Behind him a man seemed to be gliding toward him, though the man was much faster. The cloud finished its pass and a moonbeam struck the other man. The fgure flinched, as though the illumination was too bright to endure. The pistol in his hand glinted.

Lena screamed, hating herself as she yelled the cliché, "Look out! He has a gun!" She kicked off her heels and pulled her small, lightweight, revolver from her purse—her father had given it to her—before shedding the purse and her cloak as well. She grabbed a handful of her dress and sprinted toward Derrick, cursing her dress, and cursing Derrick as well, for not carrying the Glock she had given him for his birthday.

The other man saw her draw her gun and stopped. For a moment she thought he would flee, but instead he planted his feet and fired off six rapid shots from an impossible distance. Derrick fell to the ground in a puff of snow. Lena shrieked with rage as she unloaded her gun at the stranger. However, if the stranger's shots had been impossible, hers were even more so. The futility of her situation made her scream all the louder. The man fled, unharmed.

When Lena got to Derrick's side it was too late. Part of

her mind had known that when she'd seen him fall, but she had succumbed to the blind rage that always followed on the heels of someone hurting her family. She rolled him onto his back and promptly vomited in the snow next to him, dry heaving until she could look at him again. His handsome face was ruined. Tears streaked down her face, each one colder than the last, echoing the cold fury that was building inside her.

She looked up toward the giant oak toward which the figure had fled. "I will find you!" She promised, "I will find you, and then I will destroy you—you and anyone else who had a hand in this."

In her anger, she forgot her irritation toward Derrick for bringing her here, she forgot how tired she was of his sloppy, uncouth ways, the way he had touched her as if she were a toy made for his pleasure, and even how she had begun to dread seeing him. Her mind only remembered the good times—brief as they had been—and that he was hers. Lena touched Derrick's hair tenderly, "What did you do, Derrick?"

The harsh cry of sirens brought her out of her rage. She had to get out of there. If nothing else, she didn't want the first thing people heard about her new publishing company to be that it was associated with a murder.

She quickly gathered her belongings: shoes, ruined; cloak, ruined; purse, ruined; revolver, functional but in need of cleaning—and hightailed it back to her car. She drove quietly out a back road, carefully going the speed limit all the way back to her house. It was difficult to drive at first. Once in the safety of her car she began to feel how cold her feet were, how sluggish and floppy from the biting cold of the snow.

By the time she arrived home, the shock of the night was beginning to set in and she was exhausted. She stripped her torn and bloody clothes from her body, dropping them in a pile on the bathroom floor before stepping into the shower. She scrubbed until the water stopped running pink with Derrick's blood and then she scrubbed longer, as if by scrubbing off her skin she could wash away the horror of the night's events.

Finally, she collapsed at the bottom of her shower, shaking and crying. She was so used to being in control that she didn't have the slightest idea how to deal with being out of control. She sobbed for a long while before she could pull herself together enough to form a plan. She coughed and cleared her throat. Even in the heart of darkness, there are options. With this thought, she stood up, turned off the shower and began to make a list of her options.

"Option one: I could let the police take care of it. However, the best way to do that would have been to stay with...the body...until they came. Now it will look like I did it. Plus, it would be bad for business."

"Option two: I could hire someone else to look into it. Of course the cops have better access to resources than a PI. Besides, my involvement would still be revealed.

"Or I could do what I can, myself. While it's true, I won't have access to the same resources, I would be able to talk to Derrick's friends, who wouldn't speak to the police."

She liked feeling she'd actually be doing something instead of just waiting for someone else to tell her about it. It put some control back into her hands. Her need for independence was why she had started her publishing company in the first place, after all. After she'd made her decision, Lena built a fire and burned the clothes she'd worn that night. When the last shred of cloth had been consumed by flame, she lay down to sleep. It was nearing seven in the morning, so she set her alarm for eleven, falling asleep almost as soon as she lay down.

*　　*　　*

WHEN HER ALARM blared her into consciousness she jerked awake, the cogs of her mind began to turn, and she remembered the night's events: the party, the text from Derrick, and finally Derrick's death. She shuddered and gagged, remembering the shattered remains of his face. Lena pressed her hand to her heart, in a feeble attempt to keep it from beating out of her chest. She was shaking and covered in a cold sweat when she finally crawled out of bed to the shower.

"Okay," she said to her cat, Khan, who was happily licking the shower curtain. "First, I'm going to drive over to Derrick's place and see if the police have already been there. If they have, then I'll try to track down some of his friends. If they haven't, I'll search through it to see what I can find."

When she went down to her garage she saw that her

car was a mess. In the dark and as filled with fear as she had been, she hadn't noticed how covered in blood she had been. Derrick's blood was smeared across the steering wheel and on the dials. She shuddered, thinking about cleaning it up. "But if I don't, when the police come to investigate me—and they will —they'll find it."

Lena gritted her teeth, went back inside for soap, water, bleach, and towels, grateful that she had decided to read Derrick's crime novels, one of which told how to clean up a murder scene. Soon the car was clean and smelled only of bleach. She took out the old air freshener and put a new one in. Her next stop was the car wash.

Finally, she drove over to Derrick's house.

There were no police cars loitering out front, nor caution tape strung up. Convenient as it was for her purposes, she felt strangely betrayed that the authorities that were supposed to "protect and serve" hadn't even arrived yet. It only solidified her desire to fnd and punish Derrick's murderer. Never mind that she had been ready to break up with him. He was still hers. And her Derrick had been stolen from her before she could send him away.

Lena let herself in through the unlocked back door. His was the standard filthy house of a bachelor. She'd only made minimal progress in getting him to clean up after himself, which is why they spent most of their time at her house.

He had changed the décor since she'd last been there.

Derrick had always been whimsical and eccentric. It had been something she had found attractive about him. But it was clear that the whimsy had been lost—swallowed up by something much, much darker. Gone were the brilliant colors and fantastical prints of exotic lands. These had been replaced by darkness and gloom. The display of tickets to the Trans-Siberian Orchestra—one of their first dates—were replaced with strange sounding gothic industrial bands. Bands she had never heard of, let alone been invited to attend with him. His walls were plastered with pictures of vampire porn and pictures of him with beautiful men and women. His desk was littered with fake fangs and claws, his bookshelf now held books on the occult instead of standard fantasy novels. And the room was filled with Club Pandemonium paraphernalia.

Sure, she'd known he had friends who worked at Club Pandemonium, that he went there a lot and that it was vampire-themed, but why was he even dating her if their interests had become so contrary? She had believed Club Pandemonium was somewhere he went on the weekends with his buddies. But this was his life, it seemed—a life that he never spoke to her about. When she looked in the closet, she was glad he hadn't shared. The instruments of torture she found would have horrified her—did horrify her.

Part of her wanted to scream *Fuck you, Derrick!* and run. But although his death had exposed his infidelity, dishonesty, and cruelty, she had promised him vengeance. And his being a liar, a cheat, and a coward didn't give anyone the right to murder him.

Lena angrily made copies of some of the photos, slamming them down onto the printer: pictures of him with people he seemed most at ease with. People who weren't her. When she went to Club Pandemonium, these would be the people she would look for, the ones who would have the most insight into his secret life.

She left things as Derrick had left them—semi-organized in some logic foreign to her—before returning home. She would need specialized clothing to be allowed into the club. The clothes in Derrick's closet all had tags from Octane, a costume shop downtown.

✿　✿　✿

THE DRIVE TO Octane was uneventful. She turned on the radio, hoping to hear something about Derrick's murder, but there was nothing. She found that strange—like the lack of police presence at Derrick's house. It was frustrating. As if no one had noticed his death. She knew the police had come to the scene—she had heard the sirens approaching—and with that there should have been something on the news. If by some odd chance Derrick hadn't had his license on him, there would have at least been a call to identify his body.

When she arrived at Octane, she found there were no parking spaces free, which though not unusual in Columbus, irked her. The five-block walk was through a disgusting blend of slush and filth. The slush, in combination with the overcast skies, darkened Lena's mood further until she was cursing her high-priced designer shoes with each tug that pulled them out of the muck. She landed on Octane's doorstep in a foul mood.

Octane's sign was made from oversized nuts and bolts. Very industrial. With an irritated flick of her head she tossed her hair over her shoulder and pondered how to deal with the staff. There was no way she could pass for a regular patron. But perhaps it would work to come off as stupid and rich. Lena pasted a vapid look on her face and pushed open the door.

The front room was flled with what could be Halloween costumes, most of the women's wear called "Sexy" something. A man dressed in black leather that could have come straight out of Derrick's closet came over immediately. His face was pale and sickly looking, as if he hadn't seen the sun in years. There were dark rings around his eyes, made more obvious by the heavy black make-up he wore.

"Can I help you?" His voice rasped as if he had just smoked two packs of cigarettes and his eyes were bloodshot. He also reeked. Given his greasy hair, it had probably been a few days since water had made contact with it. At least Derrick had bathed.

Lena tried not to wrinkle her nose or gag. Instead she looked up at him and fluttered her eyelashes, "Oh, yes! My boyfriend invited me to Club Pandemonium tonight—he goes there, like, all the time—but I've never been, and anyway, he told me to come here to get the right clothes but I just don't know what to get and would you please help me?"

"Uh? Club Pandemonium? You're going there?" The salesman squinted at the Sexy Huntress outfit Lena was standing in front of. "You won't be able to get in with any of this crap. These are Halloween costumes. You'll want Rafe to show you the back room." He called over his shoulder, "Rafe! Fresh blood for the club!"

Lena blinked and a young man seemed to materialize before her. Rafe had the natural allure that the other man was trying to imitate with make up and avoidance of the sun. Unlike the other man, Rafe looked healthy. He was also blindingly handsome—like the people in Derrick's photographs.

"My dear," Rafe said bowing over her hand, "please let me show you what we have."

He led Lena into the basement. When he flipped on the light, Lena had to smother a gasp. These clothes were aggressive in their promiscuity and in their domination—fit only for porn. But he didn't stop. "My dear, people like you and I wouldn't be caught dead in such trash, would we?" To which Lena could only smile, relieved that she wouldn't have to wear something so ostentatious and frankly, disturbing. She continued to follow him to the rearmost section. Lena hadn't realized the store extended so far. Here, the clothes were reminiscent of the Victorian Era, yet clearly their own style: corsets, top hats, pipes, great cloaks, long coats, shoes, and so on—but just a little off. The slits in the skirts were a bit too high, the necks definitely too low. Some of the clothes were decorated with gears and little bits of machinery.

"These are lovely." Lena whispered touching a burgundy colored steel-boned corset.

Rafe smiled gently, "Many of us grew up wearing similar clothing, and though we cannot reconcile it with who we are now, we can at least bring a measure of their romanticism to life." He pulled out a black skirt that went fetchingly with the corset Lena was touching, "These days we call it steampunk." Rafe helped her pick an outfit, and then, because it was all so lovely, a third and fourth as well. "I believe I overheard you saying you would be going to Club Pandemonium tonight?"

"Yes I am." She wasn't certain how he could have overheard that bit of conversation, but she also wasn't certain how he had appeared so quickly before her when she hadn't even seen him.

Rafe nodded to himself, "Well, your boyfriend seems to have kept you very uninformed. Tonight is the Yuletide Masquerade. It's a rather impressive night, even for Club Pandemonium. While these are lovely, and would be, on almost any other night, quite appropriate, for tonight these simply won't do."

Lena smiled, "Of course, not for a masquerade!"

He looked her over again, calculating, "I expect you want to stand out?"

Lena flushed. "Yes."

"Very well, no wolves, ravens, bats, then. No pandas either, though they're popular, given the club's name. Is there any animal you feel an affinity for?"

Lena hesitated, "I like panthers, but I expect all the girls will be dressed as some kind of sexy cat, won't they?"

Rafe practically beamed at her, "Actually, no. Most people who go to the Pandemonium tend to shun felines." He looked her up and down, evaluating her body and pose carefully, "Yes, I think that will do very well." He left her to pose before the long mirror for a moment, before reappearing with a deep red skirt embroidered with black panthers leaping and pouncing. The skirt's cloth was almost too dark to see the cats against it.

Lena beamed taking in her costume. It was perfect. For what she wasn't certain, but perfect none the less.

Rafe's eyes flicked between Lena and the looking glass, he breathed a soft sigh, "That looks like it was made for you."

Lena smiled, her eyes twinkling with amusement, "Perhaps it was."

Rafe laughed. It was a strange sound, somewhere between patronizing and ironic. "No. I made it for my little sister some time ago, but she refused to wear it. She claimed it was too loud. She was a quiet girl, more suited to matrimony than to adventure."

Lena frowned. He said 'was,' as if his sister were dead. Yet these beautiful clothes were made for a woman, not a girl, and Rafe didn't look old enough for the exchange to have been very long ago.

"No," He continued. "I think your spirit resembles my own far more than hers." He smirked. "The same kind of killer instinct, fashionably clothed and fashionably used I expect."

"Killer instinct?" Lena laughed, waving off his comment. Of course she was planning murder, once she tracked down Derrick's killer. "Please, I own a publishing company."

A sly smile crept over his face, "Anyone who owns a company has to be cutthroat." He half closed his eyes and leaned back slightly, "Anyway, all artists are demons at heart. No one can write a good story without conflict in their hearts." He ran his hand through his hair, "I once knew an author who said of himself, 'Only two kinds of people dream up murder, and I'm the one that gets paid better.'"

Lena frowned. "That's from a TV show."

Rafe shrugged. "It was an artist speaking through his puppet. Which amounts to much of the same thing."

Lena pondered his words as they looked through other skirts and corsets. That had certainly been true of Derrick. When they had first met he was a young author, mainly writing poetry and short fiction where the hero always triumphed over the darkness and good always won. But as their relationship progressed, so did his writing. The characters became more conflicted. Good didn't always win. Hell, in some of his stories good wasn't always even present. The more conflicted his stories became, the more the people demanded. The more she demanded from him as well. She had to admit that part of her anger at his death was the gap it would leave in her publishing schedule.

That realization shook her. She felt...less human. Certainly she was supposed to be angry because she loved him and he was dead—not because it was an inconvenience. Did she even love him? Guilt threatened to strangle her. Her quest for vengeance became even more important; if she didn't punish the ones that killed him, it would mean that she had never loved him. That was something she couldn't let be true. Her resolution to destroy his murderers burned anew. She would kill them because she loved Derrick—even if, in the end, he hadn't loved her back. Even if he had become twisted, her love was true, and she would follow it to its natural conclusion.

"Now," Rafe said straightening the skirt here, plucking a bit of cloth there, "I'm sure you're aware that every social group has its own rules. Well, in ours, we play for keeps."

Lena raised an eyebrow. That could mean all sorts of things, "What do you mean?"

"There are a few things you should keep in mind while you are at the club."

Lena looked at the striking costume she was wearing. "Please tell."

Rafe launched into the kind of lecture an indulgent father might give his favorite daughter. "Don't take any drinks from anyone, at any time, with the exception of the bartender, of course. But when you receive drinks from him, make certain that the drink goes from his hand to yours. Not to the counter, not to a waitress—there aren't any on the ground floor of the Club anyway—from his hand to your hand. Don't let anyone kiss you. That would be making a promise I assure you, you don't want to keep. And do not, under any circumstance, invite anyone home with you or to share a cab. Don't feel bad about saying no. No one who could hurt you would be offended by bluntness here. However, if you get into any trouble—and a pretty girl like you is bound to—just ask for my partner, Brick. He's a big softie. Tell him I sent you, and he'll take care of it."

Lena listened carefully and told him not to worry. Then Rafe packed her purchases up in chic boxes. He paused. "I forgot to ask you, what's your boyfriend's name? It's totally inappropriate that he didn't warn you about the club before sending you here. Someone should take him out back and beat him."

Lena froze. A cold chill crept up her spine as she remembered Derrick's shattered face against the snow. Her fury at finding his porn collection burned in her face. "You'd be too late. Derrick was murdered last night, and tonight I'm going to find out who did it and why. Then I'm going to kill them."

An amused expression crossed his face. "Do you even know what kind of people you're up against?"

Her voice was cold as a crypt. "What do you know?"

Rafe smiled. His teeth were perfectly white and perfectly sharp. "My dear, I know a few things about your Derrick. For instance, he only bought trashy clothes. The kind of clothes a man buys if he wants everything to be taken from him." He shrugged, "But obviously someone took a shine to him. I can't possibly understand why. Men who dress like trash are trash."

Lena whispered, "He was smart, and kind...at first. It almost made up for everything else."

Rafe got a thoughtful look on his face. "Hmm. Well,

someone important must have liked him to approve something like that."

"Something like what?" When Rafe didn't reply, she asked, "If they liked him, why would they kill him?"

Rafe opened his mouth to speak, then seemed to think better of it. He shrugged again, "Maybe someone found out he was two-timing his girlfriend? The older members of the club don't like cheaters very much. Many of them believe that if you can cheat on your lover then you have loyalty to no one but yourself." Rafe gave her a gentle smile as he stared into her eyes, "I think you should carry on your hunt elsewhere."

She nodded slowly. Her limbs felt strangely heavy. "I will go hunt elsewhere."

"And don't forget what I told you."

"I will not forget." Lena murmured.

"Good. Have fun tonight, my dear pussycat."

As Lena walked outside, the crisp air jolted her awake. She paused. Why had she left so suddenly? She still had so many questions. And yet she couldn't convince herself to return to Octane. The burden of her pleasantly wrapped parcels urged her toward her vehicle.

Lena continued to listen to the news throughout her drive home. The persistent silence on the subject of Derrick's murder fed into her irritation until something in her mind finally clicked. "There will probably be some news online." She thought tapping her fingers on the steering wheel, "Perhaps because the holidays are coming up, they don't want to spoil the mood with news of murder. I suppose." Her conclusion didn't totally clear her suspicion, but it was better than nothing.

She pulled into her garage and dropped her bags off in her room before booting up her laptop. She had a few of the better local news websites bookmarked, so it didn't take her long to search them all and find that there was no mention of a murder—any murders—on that Saturday. There had been a shootout on the west side where some idiot tried to kidnap his ex-girlfriend, and a fire in Gahanna that claimed the lives of a family. But there was nothing about a murder. In fact, according to the news, that part of town had been totally quiet that night.

She sat at her table for a long time, frantically trying to find any mention of his murder. Lena had been there for quite a while before Khan kneaded her leg, demanding affection.

"Ow!" She picked the cat up and put him on her lap. She scratched his head while her brain worked overtime. "Now Khan, it's important that the police are silent. It means one of three things. First, they would only keep it quiet if they thought someone very important and powerful were behind this. Second, the police could be involved, though still, I would expect someone to come make me disappear—unless he texted other people as well." Lena paused, scratching Khan harder until he yowled. "Third...I suppose...but this is probably the least probable of the three possibilities...that the body and crime could have been cleaned up and removed. I don't see how someone could do that though. The police arrived shortly after I left and I didn't see anyone except the murderer—and he ran away."

Lena paused her petting to think. Khan took offense and nipped her hand until she resumed.

"The only problem with the frst and second possibilities is that no one has come to find me. True, my cell phone was soaked in the snow and is now useless." She paused and wrote herself a note—get new phone—before continuing her train of thought. "But they would still want, no, need to find and deal with me." She shivered. This was so much more of a problem than it had been earlier. "Since no one has come for me, it's possible that sometime after I left and before the police arrived, someone cleaned the garden to the point that no one thought a crime had been committed."

Khan rolled across her lap in pleasure, almost falling off in the process.

Lena smiled down at her cat as she continued to talk things out. "If that's true then it shows a great deal of planning, and either money or influence or more likely both. The killer had to have lackeys to do some of the work, because there was a lot to clean up. Removal of...the body...and the bloody snow. So..." She tried to think of how many people it would take to do that, "At least three people dedicated to the murderer, probably more, given how quickly it was done. Also, it means that something about his body could link him to the killers, otherwise, why would they bother taking it and covering the whole thing up? It would have been easier to just pin it on me, after all. I fired my gun also." With a grimace she realized that if the murderer had used a revolver as well, it would be very difficult to prove her innocence. "Something about the body must be important."

Lena paused again, trying to remember his body in as much detail as possible. She had stroked his hair after he was shot. His hair had looked almost mahogany in color, between the blood and the moonlight shadow. Lena focused her mind, not on the sorrow she had felt as she touched his hair, but on what her senses had picked up in that moment. The air had been frigid and burned as she breathed it in. Her breath had practically crystallized when she breathed out. Aside from everything else, that was how she had known Derrick was dead after she reached him. There was no cloud of frosty breath. The cold had been so powerful and so clear it was difficult to smell much, but the stink of Derrick's blood was metallic and strong. Lena shivered. She would never forget that smell.

When her fingers had first brushed his hair there had still been some in his body. But after his heart failed, his skin had cooled, and the blood had crystallized around her fingers and under her nails. As her fingers had brushed his neck, she thought she'd felt puncture wounds. At the time she'd thought the wounds were from shrapnel—from one of the bullets that hadn't found its mark. She began to scratch Khan's head in earnest. Had Derrick been doing drugs? If so, it couldn't have been for long. She'd have noticed. Or would she?

But...track marks on his neck?

Lena got up from the couch and put the kettle on. Why had he called her that night at all, knowing how important the party had been to her? There were only two reasons she could think of: he was breaking up with her or he needed cash to bail himself out of a bind. If he'd needed cash, then his very influential murderer—his drug dealer?—would have waited for him to get the money from her, or would have tried to intimidate her with threats.

Lena closed her eyes, remembering the cold chill that had raced up her spine when the murderer had looked at her before fleeing. She quivered. He wanted me to see Derrick die. Why? He wouldn't do that if he were trying to get money from me. So did Derrick call me to the garden at four in the morning to break up with me? Then someone else took that opportunity to murder him? She shook her head and poured the hot water in with her tea. Someone who knew Derrick well —well enough to know he was meeting me there, when I had only found out a little before.

Her hand clenched around her mug. "Then it had to be someone he knew from the club." A single tear struggled before running down her cheek. A jealous lover perhaps? Someone who was angry that he had been dating me, or someone who didn't think he was actually breaking up with me?

She sipped her tea, not bothering to acknowledge the tear by wiping it away. "No. That doesn't make sense. If it was a jealous lover, well, six shots is overkill. Also, if I had killed him, he would have been looking me in the face when he died." She took another sip, "So if it wasn't a lover, I just don't know."

Lena felt wounded, lost, and hopeless. *I don't want to go to a strange club with a bunch of weirdoes that think they are in some sort of fantasy world.* She ran her hand through her hair. *But I made a promise and I'm going to follow it through.* Her declaration of honor was hollow, even to her ears. This wasn't about Derrick anymore—if it ever had been. This was about someone stealing what was hers. This was about her growing desire to unravel the mystery. Lena pushed the thoughts away and struggled to believe she was doing this all for her lover. "I am a good person."

Her lack of sleep was catching up with her. She set her alarm so that she would have the maximum amount of sleep before arriving at Club Pandemonium at exactly eleven o'clock. The limo company promised her a car by ten-thirty sharp. She'd done all she could. She slept deeply and at ease knowing things would be ready when she woke.

❈   ❈   ❈

WHEN THE ALARM blared—startling Khan, who ran under the bed—Lena sprang out of bed and into action. As she dressed, she thanked her father for being a paranoid, wealthy man. For her thirteenth birthday he had given her what amounted to a chastity knife. It was thin and small, designed to go under a skirt. She put it on under her Victorian costume, attaching it to a garter high on her thigh.

Her revolver, another present from her father, she

found cleaned in her gun case. She couldn't remember cleaning it, but her father had drilled her so hard that you never put a gun away dirty that she wasn't surprised that she had done it and then forgotten. She loaded it and put it in her purse with her wallet. I never thought it was a good idea to let people carry firearms into bars, she thought. Even if they aren't allowed to drink. But now I'm glad that law slipped through.

At ten thirty, Lena stepped out of her house and carefully locked the door behind her. The driver helped her into the back with little more than, "Evening miss."

Lena was pleased that she wouldn't have to speak with anyone. She used her time commuting to the club to form the beginning of a plan. She would look for the people in Derrick's photos and question them as best she could. She couldn't force anyone to answer her questions, but she hoped she could at least trick them into it. It wasn't perfect, but it was the best she could come up with.

She was so focused on her plan that she didn't notice the limo pass by the back entrance to Club Pandemonium. Even if she'd been looking out the window, Lena probably would have missed it anyway. The back entrance was tucked around the corner and shrouded in darkness. The hum of the pulsating music Lena took to be the rumble of the limousine, so she didn't glance up at all. If she had, she would have seen a throng of people wearing clothes from Octane that Rafe had dismissed as the kind of clothes people wear when they are trash or want everything taken from them.

If she had seen them, she would have felt sorry for them. The men and women were practically naked; many wearing metal collars and steel spikes—things that only drew the cold closer to them. However, whatever compassion Lena would have felt would have done nothing for them, nor her. She wouldn't have stopped for them. Rafe had been right when he called those people trash. After all, Derrick had been one of them and he was nothing but a dog.

When the limousine turned the corner, Lena gasped at Club Pandemonium's main entrance. It was a beautiful blend of Victorian, Gothic and modern styles. Towers perforated the sky, some seeming to rise to impossible heights. The courtyard was walled with great black stones that looked like they had been there for centuries.

The driver slowed to follow a horse-drawn carriage to the entrance. It was clear that someone must have swept away the snow from the stairs, though it looked as if the snow had simply bowed to the will of Club Pandemonium and fallen around the path. Lena gawked for a moment at the elegant costumes of the other guests. It had been years since she had seen quality like this.

The club's main entrance seemed like the beginning to a dark and beautiful fairytale. Gargoyles stood or crouched proudly, their wicked faces mocking the garlands of holly leaves and berries around their brows. Great icicles hung like spears. It should have been terrifying. But the air hummed with anticipation, not fear, and that was answered by Lena's own anticipation of the end of her quest.

A knight, his armor blackened as if by smoke, handed Lena out of the limousine. The pattern of flame licking his armor was mesmerizing. Tearing her eyes away from him, she thanked him before proceeding through the doors as if she did this every day. Her belly quivered with anticipation and fear. If whoever had murdered Derrick and covered up the crime were here, they would be powerful and protected. She began to realize just how terrible an idea this was.

Rafe seemed to believe she would fit with these people. But Lena was having second thoughts. The music was both familiar and completely foreign—equal parts beautiful and disturbing. She could hear the background singers singing in Latin, she could see the rock band behind them. She couldn't shake the feeling that someone was hissing something terrible and destructive, yet wherever she turned, she couldn't find the lead singer.

Just when she was about to clasp her hands over her ears and scream, the sound stopped and she saw a man standing in front of her. He was wearing a jackal mask, his clothes a strange blend of ancient Egyptian and Victorian. "Can I buy you a drink?" He extended an elegant arm for her.

Lena shivered, something about the way his eyes glowed behind his mask creeped her out, "No...no, but thank you. I think I need to sit down." She didn't mention that she couldn't drink because she was carrying. Instead she looked around the room—which was essentially a ballroom—but saw nowhere to sit. The space was taken up with people and yuletide decorations. "Could you tell me where I could sit down?"

His eyes gleamed behind his jackal mask. "I'll do you one better and show you." He led her through the crowd to a large and elegant staircase. "The council that owns the club refuses to put in seating on the first floor. They seem to believe that humans will dance longer and drink more if they cannot rest. I suppose it works, since they keep begging to come back, but it still seems uncharitable to me."

The closer they got to the stairs, the further they got from the strange rock band and the louder the blaring gothic industrial music from the other part of the club became. With the harsh music pounding in her head and making her fingers tingle, Lena had a hard time following the jackal's words, "Did...did you say 'humans'?"

"Of course! Who else would that mess be for?" He gestured toward the swarm of leather-covered bodies that could just be seen through a door someone had carelessly left open.

Lena shook her head. It seemed strangely fuzzy. "What did you say your name was?"

He laughed. "My apologies! I completely forgot to introduce myself! My name is Jack." He pointed at his mask. "Which is why I'm wearing a jackal mask. Clever, huh?"

Lena didn't think it was particularly clever, but by now

her knees felt like jelly and all she wanted to do was sit. She struggled to remember how to stand. "How far to those chairs?"

Jack lifted his mask, revealing one of the painfully beautiful faces from Derrick's photographs. "Do you want me to take you to your house? Or call you a cab?" His eyes danced with something dark.

He was a terrible actor. He couldn't conceal the danger in his eyes, and his concern was unconvincing. "Uh, no. My driver is waiting outside. I'm sure I'll be fine." Lena struggled to remember where they were headed and not to laugh. "But a chair would still be lovely."

Jack frowned. "Very well." He led her promptly to a chair at the top of the stairs, and then turned as if to leave her.

"Jack?" Lena struggled with her handbag.

"Yes?" He turned back hungrily, his carefully polished nails burrowing into his palms.

"Do you know this man?" Lena handed him the photo she had found in Derrick's room of Derrick and Jack at what looked like a concert.

Jack glowered. "Where did you get this?"

Lena waved his anger away with one hand. "It isn't important." She fixed her eyes on Jack—a little unsteadily—but fixed nonetheless. "How do you know Derrick?"

He shrugged. "We had an understanding of sorts. He

gave me what I wanted and I gave him what he wanted."

Her voice lowered threateningly. "Sex."

Jack either didn't hear the warning in her voice, or didn't care. He shrugged. "Among other things, of course."

"Of course." She put the photo away. "What do you know of his murder?"

Jack threw his head back and laughed. It seemed he had been practicing on how to laugh like a jackal barks, and that bothered Lena deeply. "He was hardly murdered."

Lena slammed her fist on the table. "Don't lie to me! I was there! I held his corpse after the life left it!" Her voice had risen and people were looking at them. Young and beautiful people whose eyes held no sympathy. In fact, few of them seemed to even hold life.

Jack glanced down at her smugly. "I also saw him fall in the snow, and I assure you, he and I walked back into the club together."

Lena gasped, shaking her head. *I saw him fall.* His words echoed in her mind. "You were the gunman, weren't you? There was only Derrick, the gunman and myself."

Jack smiled wickedly without answering her question. "I spoke to him this evening. He is very hungry, but otherwise, quite well. I assure you."

Lena jumped to her feet. "You lie!"

He shrugged. "I can show you." He stood. "Follow me

if you like."

Lena struggled with her emotions. This was obviously a trap, but it might give her some information. Her muddled brain struggled to find a reason not to go, but Jack was looking at her with the same piercing eyes Rafe had. She found herself following Jack, but she couldn't remember when she started, only that now they were stepping out of an elevator onto a plush red carpet. Turkish? The wall helpfully told her she was 'HERE' on floor six — she hadn't thought the floors went up that high — and she was led to a room locked like a maximum-security jail cell.

The jackal — Jack, she reminded herself with a giggle — told her to open the door. When she did — it seemed to take such a long time to do so — Derrick was standing in the middle of the room. His face wasn't the ruined hole it had been this morning — only this morning? — it was whole. Whole and flawless. Gone were the acne scars and the jagged scar he had across his cheek from a drunken night. He looked just like the people in his photographs. The glow of life had faded from him as well. It was creepy.

"Derrick?" Her voice shook.

Derrick's eyes slid over to her, taking her in. He inhaled deeply through his nostrils. "Lena, you smell fantastic. I...you've never smelled so good before." He took a step forward.

Jack leaned casually against the door, effectively

blocking Lena's escape. "Derrick, your girlfriend came all this way to make sure you're well. Why don't you show her how good you're feeling?"

Lena shook her head, trying to clear the cobwebs that clung to her mind. "But...but I saw you get shot. I know you died." She rounded on Jack. "Did you shoot him? Was that you?"

A wicked grin speared across Jack's face. "I may have shot him, but he doesn't seem to have come to any harm."

Lena shrieked. She didn't understand how Derrick could be on his feet now, when he had been clearly dead, but she had found his killer. She pulled out her gun and shot Jack in the chest in one swift motion.

Jack backhanded her, sending her flying across the room. He fingered the hole Lena's bullet had put in his shirt. "I liked this costume!" He turned on Lena, who was struggling to stand after hitting her head against the wall. "Derrick, why don't you have a little snack?"

Derrick took another step toward Lena, this time stretching his muscles as iflike he had just awoken from a long sleep. "I wanted to tell you, about all this, really I did. You had always encouraged me to be better. But you treated me like crap, Lena! I'm worth so much more than you could imagine. I am so much more than you could dream of." He strode across the rest of the distance and knelt beside Lena, pushing her down even as he gathered her up in his arms.

Every time she tried to struggle, she thought she'd vomit. Red-hot panic raced up her spine. She couldn't resist Derrick as he held her arms down. He smiled, revealing gleaming white fangs.

"Fangs?" She whimpered helplessly. Her vision blurred, maybe it was the blow to her head, but suddenly monsters seemed so much more real than before. "I always thought monsters were a-ah-fairytale." She slurred.

Jack smiled benevolently at her confusion. "And we have worked very hard to keep fools like you believing that. Please don't feel bad that you fell for it. Some of us have had centuries of practice manipulating events. There's no way a child could have seen through it."

Derrick didn't acknowledge Jack's comment. He was too busy rubbing his face in Lena's hair. "I always loved the smell of your hair, but now," he slid his mouth toward her neck. "This is so much more compelling." He bit into her neck.

She thrashed, the haze of confusion forced away by the blaze of fear that swept over her. Her mind raced a mile a minute, carefully logging everything she had done that evening and asking, *Where was your brain for this?* A helpless portion of her mind screamed. *Derrick! Derrick! Please stop!* Even as the rest of it ridiculed her for asking him to stop while he was chewing on her neck. No—not chewing—drinking her blood.

As Jack smiled down at them, like he was watching his newborn son for the frst time, Lena struggled with her thoughts. Vampires? She had always thought they were a myth. Then she remembered Rafe's strange warnings. Hadn't she always heard you had to invite vampires into your house? Couldn't they turn into bats, rats and wolves? That would explain those costumes as more than an animal of choice. It was becoming harder to think as Derrick sucked away at her neck.

"What was the last thing Rafe had said? Ask for Brick?" She murmured softly as her energy was being quickly sapped.

Jack's eyes widened with fear, but he didn't move.

Lena's voice was weak. She couldn't even hear herself over the sound of Derrick's slurping. Her life drained away. "Brick. I want Brick. Rafe told me to ask for Brick."

Suddenly Jack slapped Derrick off Lena with one clean swipe of his hand. Derrick's teeth shredded her neck further as they pulled away. Mist rose up from the floor, forming itself into a formidable olive-skinned man. He was easily six and a half feet tall, probably taller, and dressed like some sort of Persian warrior god.

"Who called for me?" His eyes were hard as granite and the grey of storm clouds.

Lena thought the whole situation—what situation was that again?—quite funny and giggled a sort of sick bubbling sound. She could hear voices, but she had gone past the point where she could distinguish them without focusing, and focusing was so very hard. She seemed to float for a long time before the olive-skinned man — Brick, her mind chirped in helpfully — knelt over her.

His face seemed to glow harshly above hers. "Do you want to live?"

Lena's voice was unsteady and weak. "I don't want to die."

A measure of sadness came into his eyes. "We all die eventually. What I want to know is if you want to live now."

"Yes," she whispered the last of her strength failing.

When Lena woke up, Rafe's face was over hers and he was grinning. "I told you pretty girls always get into trouble."

She grimaced sitting up. "I feel...." She hesitated. "Wonderful?"

Rafe smiled. "Thirsty?"

She nodded. "Now that you mention it, yes. Very."

He handed her a glass of red wine. "You'll get used to that eventually." He glanced at Brick, who was reclining on a chair sulkily. "At least that's what I've been told."

Lena raised an eyebrow at his comment before sipping the wine cautiously. It was sweet. "Red wine isn't normally this sweet." Her eyes slid toward the morose giant. He still managed to look ominous, in spite of the childishly grumpy look on his face.

Rafe shrugged. "Your palate has changed. That's blood."

She eyed the glass with horror and though she longed to throw it to the ground, she found that she was too thirsty to stop drinking it for long. She felt sick to her stomach.

Rafe smiled. "Don't worry. It isn't human blood. I didn't think you would be able to deal with the idea of drinking human blood the same day you learned that vampires are real."

"That was kind of you." She murmured, staring at the glass of unknown animal blood. In some ways, it was worse to be drinking the blood of an animal. At least with a human, you could pick bad ones or villains. An animal had no choice. She sighed heavily. "So, I'm dead then?"

Rafe stretched. "Mostly."

"And Derrick and Jack? Are they dead?" Lena grimaced as she took another sip. She was disgusted by how delicious it tasted and by how compelled she felt to continue drinking it. If this was how Derrick had felt when she walked into his room, she could understand why he'd jumped her. If her best friend walked through the door, she wouldn't be able to stop herself from pouncing.

Brick nodded, frowning. "Our law, your law now as well, decrees that if a vampire—Derrick—attacks someone—you—under the protection of a more powerful vampire—me—it is that vampire's duty to execute them. If I hadn't slain

Derrick, I would have forfeited my position to him." Brick cracked his knuckles. "I don't like to kill. When you get to be my age, you'll understand." He seemed to drift off for a moment before continuing. "Anyway, the laws must be followed, or everything we have built will fall apart."

Rafe shook his head. "I still think some mercy isn't a bad thing. The kid fell in with a bad vampire. He may not even have known the rules."

Brick cut him off, though he never raised his voice. "No. If you bend the rules for one then everyone wants a special favor."

Rafe shrugged. "Anyway, that's why Derrick is dead, really dead. Jack encouraged him to break the law, so he'll be put on trial before the Council. At worst, he'll be imprisoned for a few hundred years."

Lena felt anger burn inside her. As well as a sudden, unexpected pang of sympathy for Derrick. "So Jack almost got me killed, but he didn't die, and Derrick did? That sounds a little unfair."

Rafe sighed. "Life isn't fair Lena. You should know that. This, like life, is unfair as well."

Lena glowered.

"Look," Brick said standing up. "Derrick's murderer— as you believed him—will be punished. The man that cheated on you—yes, everyone knew about that—is dead. If you want to kill me for putting Derrick down, or Rafe for not telling you what we are, fine. But wait a thousand years so you have a chance." The disdain in Brick's voice made it clear he didn't think a thousand years would help. Then he walked over to Rafe, kissed his upturned face and disappeared in a cloud of smoke.

Lena wanted to be angry at Brick for the callous way he had spoken, but she found she couldn't. Maybe she would get revenge on Jack, but then again, why? Jack had tricked her, and yes, almost gotten her killed, but he seemed more like the average jerk than someone she really needed to contend against. As it turned out, he hadn't taken Derrick away from her; Derrick had done that himself. Even still, she felt uncomfortable with Brick's bluntness, so instead of replying she eyed Rafe with a small grin. "Tender-hearted, you said? Loves the underdog? Are you sure you were talking about Brick?"

Rafe chuckled. "If he didn't like you, he wouldn't have saved you." He glanced wistfully at the trail of smoke still curled at the door. "Brick has a hard time expressing his emotions. I imagine that's why he likes me so much." He winked at Lena. "I don't have that problem."

Lena glowered at the smoke, watching it finish creeping under the door before she turned her eyes on Rafe. "I want to know the rules."

Rafe sighed, as if he were disappointed before smiling brilliantly and answering. "That won't be a problem."